Business As Usual

Also published by Handheld Press

HANDHELD CLASSICS
1 *What Might Have Been. The Story of a Social War*, by Ernest Bramah
2 *The Runagates Club*, by John Buchan
3 *Desire*, by Una L Silberrad
4 *Vocations*, by Gerald O'Donovan
5 *Kingdoms of Elfin*, by Sylvia Townsend Warner
6 *Save Me The Waltz*, by Zelda Fitzgerald
7 *What Not. A Prophetic Comedy*, by Rose Macaulay
8 *Blitz Writing. Night Shift & It Was Different At The Time*, by Inez Holden
9 *Adrift in the Middle Kingdom*, by J Slauerhoff, translated by David McKay
10 *The Caravaners*, by Elizabeth von Arnim
11 *The Exile Waiting*, by Vonda N McIntyre
12 *Women's Weird. Strange Stories by Women, 1890–1940*, edited by Melissa Edmundson
13 *Of Cats and Elfins. Short Tales and Fantasies*, by Sylvia Townsend Warner
14 *Business as Usual*, by Jane Oliver and Ann Stafford
15 *Non-Combatants and Others. Writings Against War, 1916–1945*, by Rose Macaulay
16 *Potterism. A Tragi-Farcical Tract*, by Rose Macaulay
17 *British Weird. Selected Short Fiction, 1893–1937*, edited by James Machin
18 *Women's Weird 2. More Strange Stories by Women, 1891–1937*, edited by Melissa Edmundson
19 *There's No Story There. Wartime Writing, 1944–1945*, by Inez Holden
20 *Where Stands A Wingèd Sentry*, by Margaret Kennedy

Business As Usual

by Jane Oliver and Ann Stafford

illustrated by Ann Stafford

Introduction by Kate Macdonald

Handheld Press

Handheld Classic 14

First published in 1933 by Collins.
This edition published in 2020 by Handheld Press.
72 Warminster Road, Bath BA2 6RU, United Kingdom.
www.handheldpress.co.uk

Copyright of the novel © the Estates of Jane Oliver and Ann Stafford 1933

Copyright of the Introduction and Notes © Kate Macdonald 2020

All rights reserved. No part of this publication may be reproduced, stored in or introduced into a retrieval system, or transmitted, in any form, or by any means (electronic, mechanical, photocopying, recording or otherwise) without the prior written permission of the publisher.

The moral rights of the authors have been asserted.

ISBN 978-1-912766-18-5

5 6 7 8 9 0

Series design by Nadja Guggi and typeset in Adobe Caslon Pro and Open Sans.

Printed and bound in Great Britain by Short Run Press, Exeter.

FSC
www.fsc.org
MIX
Paper from responsible sources
FSC® C014540

Contents

Introduction, by Kate Macdonald   vii
Works published   xx

Business as Usual
    Part I – Autumn   3
    Part II – Winter   121
    Part III – Spring   191

Notes on the novel, by Kate Macdonald   237

Kate Macdonald is a publisher and a literary historian. She has published her research in a number of books, chapters and articles on twentieth-century publishing history and the book business. Her most recent book is *Rose Macaulay, Gender and Modernity* (ed. Routledge 2018).

Introduction

BY KATE MACDONALD

Business As Usual was published at the beginning of the authors' careers as two of the most prolific professional women writers of the mid-twentieth century.[1] 'Jane Oliver' was the pen-name of Helen Christina Easson Rees, née Evans (1903–1970), and 'Ann Stafford' was Anne Isabel Stafford Pedler (1900–1966). They met while working at the *Times* Book Club in London. Anne ran the export department where Helen worked: 'I was first delighted by the gaiety of her line drawings as she doodled on her blotting-pad while dictating business letters'.[2] After Helen published her first novel in 1932 they began to collaborate as authors, and developed parallel writing careers, writing light contemporary comedies together under their pen-names, and romantic fiction as 'Joan Blair', and publishing many solo works. They reached their peak in the 1950s, when Helen was lauded by the *Sunday Times* as 'one of the best living writers of historical fiction',[3] and Ann was praised by F Tennyson Jesse for her novel *Bess*.[4] Their careers lasted until their deaths in 1966 and 1970, during which time they published at least 97 novels.

This formidable output is testament to their quality as authors, and the professionalism that enabled them to make the best use of their skills to suit the reading needs of a receptive market. The particularly rich publishing climate of the 1930s, 1940s and 1950s made it possible for them to make their living as authors, publishing novels, broadcast fiction and children's fiction for nearly thirty years. Their work was regularly performed and read aloud on BBC broadcasts in the late 1930s, and they published short fiction (Helen's writing career began when she had a story accepted), and undoubtedly serialised their novels during the 'Silver Age' of the story magazines.

Jane Oliver

Helen Evans and her younger sister Mary had grown up in Newcastleton in Roxburghshire, daughters of a country doctor. Helen went to school in St Andrews in Fife, and then to a finishing school in Lausanne in 1922–23. She then went to Bedford Training College while Mary went to Oxford. Their parents were unusual for the period in investing so determinedly in their daughters' education. In the post-First World War world they may have wanted them to be equipped for a highly uncertain world, in which women were striking out in careers and social norms.

After Bedford, Helen taught as a physical education instructor at a school in Loughborough in the late 1920s. Later, she moved to London, and she, Mary and a Canadian cousin also called Helen shared rooms together as paying guests in a house in Cadogan Square. On the dustjacket of her first solo novel, *Tomorrow's Woods* (1932) Helen described herself as 'turning her hand to half a dozen trades, she has since been gymnast, masseuse, and school teacher, a writer of penny dreadfuls, a literary secretary, and worked from nine to six in a big London bookshop.' She had been the 'literary secretary' for Clemence Dane, one of the most well-known British playwrights in the 1920s and 1930s. The 'big London bookshop' was the *Times* Book Club.

Helen gave up teaching to concentrate on becoming a writer, and her partnership with Anne Pedler followed. By 1936 they had published six novels together, and six further novels separately.

Helen and Anne were photographed by Howard Coster in 1936, in a portrait now held by the National Portrait Gallery. Helen is seated on a cushion in front of the fireplace, while Anne leans over the arm of her chair to look at their manuscript on the floor. It's a portrait of collaborative working, and Helen's intent gaze is the focus, rather than the apparently blank notebook in front of them. Helen was photographed several times by Coster that year, suggesting that she was the more famous face of the writing partnership.

She learned to fly 'on a battered Moth', obtaining her Royal Aero Club Aviator's certificate in April 1937. In 1936 she wrote to a fellow pilot and writer who had 'caught so exactly the terror and loveliness of flight', John Llewelyn Rees (he also used the spelling Rhys). They fell in love and lived together, marrying in 1939. He, like Helen, was a pilot, and also an RAF officer. He was killed in August 1940 on active service in a training accident. After his death Helen became convinced that she remained in communication with him, and transcripts survive of their 'automatic writing' conversations. Spiritualism and contacts with the dead became a feature of some of her post-war fiction, particularly *Morning for Mr Prothero* (1950).

As well as her steady work as an author, Helen was a Christian, a noted volunteer, local activist and campaigner against the export of New Forest ponies and for the Red Cross. She remained close to her mother and sister into the 1950s, and to her secretary Bet Lukens, to whom she left her home in her will. In 1962 she had had the house rebuilt in brick containing a time capsule, an event filmed by Southern TV. She continued to publish her books, and David Murdoch notes that from the 1950s she wrote children's novels in parallel with adult fiction, using her meticulous research to write stories set in the same historical period, but for different readerships.

Helen and Anne founded the John Llewelyn Rhys prize from Helen's royalties in memory of her husband, as a prize for young Commonwealth authors. She and Anne administered it for some years, then handed it to the National Book League in the 1960s. Helen remained on its selection panel, only giving up her work for the prize a few weeks before her death. Half of her obituary in *The Times* was devoted to the prize and her husband's last book, *England is My Village*, which had been posthumously awarded the Hawthornden Prize in 1942. On Helen's literary career, *The Times* reported that 'she was best known for her historical fiction, which was widely popular. Her work was thoroughly researched and nicely balanced, so that the scholarship never bore heavily on the narrative. She had a great gift for catching the vigour and variety of a period, and this was particularly marked in the novels with a background in Scottish history.'[5] She had published 31 books under her own pen-name, and had co-written a further 39 with Anne.

Ann Stafford

Little is known about Anne Pedlar's early life. Her obituary notes that she had an MA and a PhD, though it is not known when she was awarded these degrees, or from which university. She had been married but had left her husband around the time that she and Helen met. Her son John Pedler was born in 1928, and was sent to the USA during the war, returning in 1943. He later worked for the Foreign Office and became an author, dying in 2018. Like Helen, Anne drove ambulances in London during the Second World War, but she made her career as a novelist, publishing 25 books under the name of Ann Stafford, and a further 39 co-written with Helen. She was active in the British Red Cross from 1939, rising to the rank of Divisional Deputy President.[6] After the war both Anne and Helen lived in Hampshire, variously living next door to each other and sharing a house in North Gorley, Fordingbridge. In Anne's last illness Helen cared for her until her death.

Business As Usual

From the biographical outlines above it seems clear that *Business As Usual* was based on Helen and Anne's working lives and personal experience. Helen's sister Mary, an Oxford graduate like Hilary, was told many times that she needed experience to get a job, but she was never offered the experience. Like Hilary she too played hockey, and like Hilary's predecessor had to leave her job due to appendicitis. Helen and Anne recreate with relish the working lives of single women in 1930s London, and the struggle to find work that was interesting, amenable and paid enough to live on. Everyman's is clearly intended to be a version of Selfridges on London's Oxford Street. Anne, in particular, would have contributed the detail of the daily routine in a busy library, and Helen gave verve to their heroine Hilary's life outside the shop: the episode of driving in a very dubious car to Devon for hiking at Easter, and then coming back to London at dawn with the milk carts, feels typical of what we know of Helen's adventurous character.

Business As Usual was reprinted within a month of publication, and was praised by Mr Selfridge himself.[7] Its title was a common catch-phrase in the period: 'business as usual' is listed nearly 2000 times for 1933 alone in the *Guardian*'s digital archive.[8] The novel is remarkable for its blending of the particular 1930s mixture of the booming department store and the venerable institution of the lending library. The *Times* Book Club was one of the 'major British circulating libraries' of the first half of the twentieth century.[9] In 1932 Q D Leavis observed that 'the *Times* Book Club and Mudie's serve the upper middle-class and Boots' the lower middle-class, while the newsagent represents the bookshop for most people'.[10]

The conflation in this period between a bookshop and a library is confusing to the modern reader, since present-day bookshops are not libraries, and modern libraries almost never sell their stock except when they need to clear their shelves of unread tomes. The important and now obsolete factor was that borrowing from a circulating library was generally not free: one subscribed to a library to gain access to its collection. Thus the social stratification of class that was enforced by personal income affected the kind of library one used, and the amount of subscription, and the quality of books, one could afford. Hilary Fane's humane reorganisation of the Everyman's Library desks is a neat indictment of this system. No longer will her poorer library subscribers have to queue in humiliation at the Fiction C desk, which dispensed only the oldest and shabbiest books. Instead all subscribers will be able to change their books at the desk for their surname's initial, in an egalitarian fashion.

The early twentieth-century library was an important book-buying customer for publishers, since libraries were used very widely. Their customers expected to be able to borrow the most recent novels, and so libraries needed to buy large numbers of multiple copies of new and standard titles, and to replace them at regular intervals as the books deteriorated in condition. Libraries could also order books to sell to their customers.

On the other side of the rather transparent line that divided the twentieth-century bookshop from the library, both small and large bookshops developed their own brand of lending or circulating libraries. Many 1930s smaller bookshops carried lending libraries in a back room, as they had done since the Victorian period. Then, the increasing levels of adult literacy had encouraged corner shops and tobacconists to invest in cheap editions that would give a steady return of a halfpenny or a twopenny fee each time a book was borrowed. Gordon Comstock's contempt for the cheap library stock in his bookshop in George Orwell's *Keep The Aspidistra Flying* (1936) conveys a particularly sour view of what reading should and could mean to people with little money and (in his view) no taste.

This was one end of the continuum of public access to reading material. At the other end were the cosmopolitan institutions represented by the central London branches of the *Times* Book Club and its competitors: Mudie's Select Circulating Library, the Harrods Library, the library of W H Smith or even Boot's Lending Library. These were highly respectable and often venerable institutions: Mudie's was centuries older than the *Times* Book Club, and both would have shared the *Times* Book Club clientele, which were: 'Clubs, Libraries and individual customers who place standing orders with us for regular supplies of the latest books [...] many of our clients find it convenient to purchase their books through us because they are stationed in remote places where they cannot obtain local supplies'.[11]

But Hilary Fane is not working in the *Times* Book Club. She finds work in Everyman's Stores, a well-known and highly reputable department store on London's Oxford Street. It has a main entrance, with 'large, buttoned men' who guard the door (21), and it has lifts, a staff canteen, a nurse, a Book Floor with a Book Department and a Library, Millinery, Haberdashery, a packing department off-site, an Inexpensive Gown Department, a Baby Linen Department and its own delivery vans and catalogues. Most importantly, it has its own big clock on the main street entrance, which clinches Everyman's identification as Selfridges. Selfridges liked the identification enough to include *Business As Usual* in its selection of Signed Copies available from its Book Department during Christmas 1933.[12]

Selfridges ought to have liked *Business As Usual* very much, since the novel exudes loyalty to the firm, and a sense of family. Everyman's is a British institution, and its component parts offer excellent commercial services to the public. Its standards and regulations are as good as the law of the country. Its community of workers can be moved around and deployed as needed, like an army or a well-trained domestic staff. Instead of a Family to obey – this is not a Great House, but a business – there is the Board of Directors, among whom was once Hilary's Uncle Tom (this casually mentioned fact should alert the reader to the Cinderella theme in the plot). To serve at Everyman's carries distinction, since its standards are so high, and its attitude to its customers is impressively respectful. One wants to shop there, which is what a successful advertising campaign should achieve. The Selfridges Book Department of its day would have been pleased to be stocking a book that resonated so strongly with its own values.

The Everyman's staff members do their best to offer good customer service, but as in all good novels of organisation and shop-floor politics, there are nuances. There is efficiency and competence, and the results can be impressive: Hilary recognises that Miss Lamb is a professional typist, with skills beyond anything she could hope to achieve herself. There is also sloppiness, inadequacy, pig-headedness and bumbling uselessness, but the novel's generosity usually finds reasons for these flaws, inviting the reader to understand and forgive, and perhaps treat shop assistants more generously in future. The authors skilfully avoid recreating the institutional atmosphere of a boarding school, despite the plaintive efforts of Sister Smith, because the young women who swarm in and out of Everyman's staff door have homes to go to, pennies to save for the gas fire, stockings to wash and friends to see. The male staff are also given rounded portraits, particularly the friendship of Mr Salt and Mr Millett. Hilary dissects their relative social positions effortlessly, so natural is it for her to place people, and to do it according to school and university. She is generous about Mr Millett's aspirational hopes, because he will clearly go far, but she can never not see his origins as a grocer's errand boy.

Standing head and shoulders above all the men of Everyman's is Michael Grant, head of Everyman's publicity and a shining epitome of masculine excellence against whom none of Hilary's male colleagues can ever compete. He is variously described by Hilary as a magnate (42), god-like (72) and a Minor Prophet (74), careful deprecations when writing to her family that do not mask her feelings. We see that he is calm, measured, with a perfectly balanced view of how to deal with all transgressions. He is sensible, has a sense of humour, is judicious, knows when to leave well alone, and knows when he has found a colleague of good sense and efficiency. He is perfectly cast as the desirable *parti* in what is effectively a workplace romance (Helen and Anne would write Mills & Boon romances successfully for nearly thirty years). But there is far more to *Business As Usual* than romance, largely due to how the story is told.

The *Guardian* review from 1933 spotted that the novel's strength is its social realistic accuracy: 'There is a type of mind which will always get more fun from prying into the raw materials of history – the documents and the letters – than it will from reading the same materials when the historian has exercised his art upon them.'[13]

This is an epistolary novel, a mode handled here with variety and a very light touch. The letters are actively enhanced rather than merely illustrated by Ann Stafford's line drawings, and by the original layout (reproduced in this edition) that simulates telegrams, in-house memoranda and private letters. The single illustration of a certificate of posting a registered packet does all the work of a letter, with satisfying economy. These communications speak through their formats as much as they do in the meaning of their content, and there is much enjoyment in imagining the receipt of these letters, memoranda and telegrams, as well as in how they were first written and sent. Imagining oneself in the minds of the characters as they choose what and how to write to whom, and in what mode, enhances the novel's liveliness.

The exposition is enjoyable as well as informative, and Hilary Fane leaps off the page from the beginning with her enthusiasm and her self-assurance. She is certainly not perfect, since she can't add up, or type efficiently and she is unable to master NEAT PRINTING. We enjoy the process of discovering how much nicer she is to Basil than he is to her: 'I don't think one enjoys "I told you so" however beautifully it's put' (21). She tells her parents things in slightly different ways than she tells them to Basil, and soon she does not tell him things at all. She offers and gives, and he does not reciprocate. Thankfully her pride will not let matters go on into abjectness. She is a fighter, a dogged and determined young woman who knows her own market value as an employee, and as a fiancée, though she struggles to avoid being demoralised.

Once Hilary earns enough she chooses to eat and live alone, rather than in the depressing Minerva Hotel, and she sees only family friends or people she knows from home or Oxford. As soon as she can afford a flat rather than a basement room she decorates it herself, and her fairy godmother-aunt furnishes it fortuitously so that the char can be reassured that Hilary is respectable and middle-class. (That one of the first things she does on achieving this level of professional independence is to engage a cleaning lady

xv

is also a class indicator.) She does not go to the pub, or the cinema, and she goes to the theatre on her own rather than joining loud parties in a music-hall. Her class is revealed through her style of living, and her tastes clarify what the reader expects of a middle-class heroine of quite good family. Hiking in Devon at Easter with a woman friend could not be more 1930s – Harriet Vane did it on her own in Dorothy L Sayers' *Have His Carcase* (1932) – yet the authors are careful to separate Hilary and Mary wandering happily on the moors in their sandshoes from the broad-beamed urban hikers who must follow maps. Driving, even in a dilapidated car, was also the correct mode of travel for Oxford graduates. Cycling was cheaper, but just a little proletarian, as Margery Allingham's depiction of Benny Konrad in her 1937 novel *Dancers in Mourning* showed.

Even when Hilary is feeling happiest with her lot she is alert to the unhappinesses of others. One of the striking aspects of this novel is the care taken to delineate the lives of single working women. Their habitats are not grim, but they're depressing. The first thing we learn about the Minerva Hotel, Hilary's first London home, is its list of rules, and the probability that its clients are likely to leave without a day's notice. Hilary's search for work is not desperate, because she does eventually find herself a clerk's post, but her struggles in learning how to negotiate with Employment Bureaux foreshadow Miss Pettigrew's miseries in Winifred Watson's *Miss Pettigrew Lives for a Day* (1938).

Hilary's first impressions of Everyman's are largely about the women: the officious Sister Smith, the herd of women typists, the ineffectual Miss Hopper, the bristling Miss Sparling. She notices the old women searching through dustbins in the lane outside, and the chars coming home at nine in the morning after making other people's breakfasts. Miss Dowland counts her time working at Everyman's by the Mondays, and lives with, and supports, her unemployed woman friend. Miss Lamb, in her mid-twenties, is hoping to marry her Boy, but Miss Watts 'doesn't seem to have a

Boy, or if she has she's more reticent about it. Perhaps at thirty-five (or thirty) financial security is the only thing that matters' (53). When *Business As Usual* was published Anne was thirty-three and Helen was thirty.

Hilary knows that she is fortunate – 'I can always run away' (67) – since she has a fiancé and parents to go, but it's important to her to prove to herself that she can support herself for a year in London. In the context of the 1930s economy, she is taking quite a risk, and perhaps this is why Helen and Anne wanted to tackle this subject. *Business As Usual* reveals much about the desperation of single women looking for work (or being happy to stay on the dole), and it is important for the success of the novel that perseverance, a sense of humour and realism about what she can accept in a job, carry Hilary through. She is lucky to find the opening at Everyman's, and she is lucky in having a temperament that allows her to work hard at tedious and inimical tasks. She also knows that this job is probably her only chance, and she is not going to abandon it. She is very aware of the struggles of less fortunately safety-netted women. When Hilary finds her basement room, formerly a kitchen, she encounters struggling genteel Anglo-Indian poverty for the first time. The cleaning woman calmly tells her off for spilling milk on the grate that any of the other girls in the house would have been glad to have had. When Hilary encounters a woman in a dire situation, she panics because she doesn't know what to do, but her first instinct is to help, and she can do this because she knows someone in greater authority with the right resources. Life is not easy for single working women, but those who have allies will thrive.

Hilary's allies are fairy godmothers emerging when her need is greatest, whether she realises it or not. Aunt Bertha's joyful discovery of Hilary behind the Library desk causes a day-long sensation for all her colleagues, some lasting bitterness from her enemies, and herself some excruciating embarrassment. But its purpose in the plot is to place her publicly in her proper social position. As the niece of one of Everyman's most valued customers she now becomes closely connected with her colleagues' need to keep the customers happy, and she must behave correctly to colleagues and customers alike. As the niece of Lady Barnley Hilary is now recognised as having the entrée to Michael Grant's social circle. More important than the effect her fifty-minute public tea-break had on her colleagues is how she handles the aftermath: she apologises to Michael formally but privately, naturally using the correct register for their class level, establishing the beginning of their courtship by correspondence. Hilary's fairy godmother has waved her wand.

Once Hilary is released from the daily niggles of servitude by being given a junior management post, she begins to fall in love with retail. The Mail Order Department is a place of wonder and complicated staffing. She survives the Christmas period, when she has to 'take the pulse of at least a dozen different departments daily ... settle disputes, administer sal volatile and good advice' (180). She marvels at the idiocy of customers, and the brilliance of the Everyman's filing system. She reorganises the library. She is heart and soul for Everyman's continuing success, to ensure that business does carry on with its usual assurance of the best for its customers, since 'Our business is your pleasure'.

Notes

1. Unless indicated otherwise, the personal information about Helen Rees and Anne Pedler was kindly supplied by David Murdoch, Helen's nephew.

2. Jane Oliver, 'Ann Stafford', *The Times*, 29 September 1966. 14.

3. Advert for Collins, *The Times*, 27 October 1955, 13.

4. Advert for Hodder & Stoughton, *The Times*, 17 July 1951, 6.

5. 'Jane Oliver Historical Novelist', *The Times*, 18 May 1970, 12.

6. Oliver 'Ann Stafford', 1966.

7. Advert for Collins, *The Observer*, 12 February 1933, 6.

8   See Newspapers.com to search the archive of the Manchester Guardian.

9   Nicola Wilson, 'British publishers and colonial editions', in *The Book World, Selling and Distributing British Literature 1900-1940*, Nicola Wilson (ed.) (Brill, 2016), 15–30, 28.

10 Q D Leavis, *Fiction and the Reading Public* (Chatto and Windus, 1932), 14.

11 Wilson 2016, 28.

12 Callisthenes, 'A Signed Copy', *The Times*, 5 December 1933, 12.

13 'Business As Usual', *The Guardian*, 11 April 1933, 12.

Works published

Jane Oliver (Helen Rees née Evans)

Those titles published by Macmillan & Co, Friday Press, Chatto, Oliver & Boyd, and Oliver & Boyd are likely to be aimed at the children's market.

Tomorrow's Woods (Collins, 1932)

Evening of a Martinet (Collins, 1934)

Barrel Organ Tune (Collins, 1935)

The Ancient Roads of England (Cassell & Co, 1936)

Mine is the Kingdom (Collins, 1937)

Not Peace but a Sword (Collins, 1939)

Queen of Tears: The Life of Henrietta Maria (Collins, 1940)

The Hour of the Angel (Collins, 1942)

In No Strange Land (Collins, 1944)

Isle of Glory (Collins, 1947)

What's History To Us (The Carnegie Dunfermline Trust, 1949)

Sing, Morning Star (Collins, 1949)

Morning for Mr Prothero (Hammond & Co, 1950)

The Lion is Come (Collins, 1951)

Crown for a Prisoner (Collins, 1953)

Young Man with a Sword (Macmillan & Co, 1955)

Sunset at Noon (Collins, 1955)

The Eaglet and the Angry Dove (Macmillan, 1957)

The Lion and the Rose (Collins, 1958)

Bonfire in the Wind (Macmillan, 1958)

Queen Most Fair (Macmillan & Co, 1959)

Flame of Fire (Collins, 1961)

The Young Robert Bruce (Max Parrish, 1962)

Faraway Princess (Macmillan, 1962)

Costume through the Centuries (Oliver & Boyd, 1963)

The Splendid Journey (Friday Press, 1963)

Watch for the Morning (Macmillan, 1964)

Alexander the Glorious (Collins, 1965)

Candleshine No More (Collins, 1967)

Charlie is my Darling (Chatto, Boyd & Oliver, 1969)

The Blue Heaven Bends Over All (Collins, 1971)

Ann Stafford (Anne Pedler)

Silver Street (Collins, 1935)

The Game and the Candle (Collins, 1936)

Pelican without Piety (Collins, 1937)

Five Proud Riders (Hamish Hamilton, 1937)

Pony for Sale (Hamish Hamilton, 1939)

It Couldn't Happen To Us (Collins, 1939)

Cuckoo Green (Collins, 1941)

Army Without Banners (Collins, 1942)

I Want To Be Happy (Collins, 1944)

Near Paradise (Collins, 1946)

Paradise Gate (Collins, 1948)

Light me a Candle (Hodder & Stoughton, 1949)

Bess (Hodder & Stoughton, 1951)

The Great Mrs Pennington (Hodder & Stoughton, 1952)

The Time It Takes (Hodder & Stoughton, 1954)

The Seventh Veil (Hodder & Stoughton, 1954)

Blossoming Rod (Hodder & Stoughton, 1955)

Seven Days Grace (Hodder & Stoughton, 1957)

The Custody of Anne (Hodder & Stoughton, 1959)

Saigon Journey (Campion Press, 1960)

A Match to Fire the Thames (Hodder & Stoughton, 1961)

It Began in Bangkok (Hodder & Stoughton, 1961)

The Age of Consent (Hodder & Stoughton, 1964)

The Young Bernadette (Max Parrish, 1965)

Bernadette and Lourdes (Hodder & Stoughton, 1967)

Jane Oliver and Ann Stafford

Business As Usual (Collins, 1933)

Cook Wanted (Collins, 1934)

Cuckoo in June (Collins, 1935)

Reluctant Adonis (Collins, 1938)

Joan Blair (Helen Rees née Evans and Anne Pedler)

Love on Wheels (Wright & Brown, 1935)

Green Eyes for Jealousy (Wright & Brown, 1936)

Two Against the World (Wright & Brown, 1936)

Sister of Nelson Ward (Mills & Boon, 1937)

Back of the Moon (Mills & Boon, 1938)

Love and Sister Lorna (Mills & Boon, 1939)

Love is Born Free (Mills & Boon, 1939)

Love is for Ever (Mills & Boon, 1940)

The Girl in the Golden Gown (Mills & Boon, 1940)

For Love Forgotten (Mills & Boon, 1941)

The Glitter and the Gold (Mills & Boon, 1941)

Let April Linger (Mills & Boon, 1942)

Love Leads to the Stars (Mills & Boon, 1942)

The Pillar of the House (Mills & Boon, 1944)

Look Again, Lovers! (Mills & Boon, 1945)

The Shadow Beside Her (Popular Fiction, 1946)

Dreams Can Come True (Mills & Boon, 1946)

Dare I Believe You? (Mills & Boon, 1948)

Tomorrow My Darling! (Mills & Boon, 1949)

Home for a Stranger (Mills & Boon, 1951)

So True to Love (Mills & Boon, 1952)

Course of True Love (Mills & Boon, 1954)

Homecoming Heart (Mills & Boon, 1954)

April Encounter (Mills & Boon, 1955)

Never A Stranger (Mills & Boon, 1956)

Beckon Me Back (Mills & Boon, 1956)

The Dominie's Lodging (Mills & Boon, 1957)

Sensible Marriage (Mills & Boon, 1957)

The Gay Adventure (Mills & Boon, 1958)

Lonely No Longer (Mills & Boon, 1959)

Leap Before you Look (Mills & Boon, 1960)

Rainbow in December (Mills & Boon, 1960)

But Goes Deeper (Mills & Boon, 1961)

Dare You Remember (Mills & Boon, 1962)

The Way to the Wedding (Mills & Boon, 1963)

Nurse Harriet Comes Home (Mills & Boon, 1964)

Note on the text

The text for this edition was created by non-destructively scanning the 1965 Library Association edition, and recreating the original layout as far as could be managed, given the slightly different page dimensions and font sizes. All the original illustrations were scanned and reinstated, and typographical errors were silently corrected. Most of the extraneous full stops were removed, and some compound nouns like 'any one' made into one word.

Business As Usual

TO

THE PEOPLE WHO

WORK

FROM NINE TILL SIX

So far as we are aware, no store called EVERYMAN's exists, in Oxford Street or elsewhere. But there are many like it.

The staff of the Book Floor live and move in our imagination only. But the originals are everywhere: they work from nine till six and have their being in the hours which remain.

J O
A S

Part I – Autumn

From the Court Column of the Daily Post, 30th July, 1931.

'Mr Rainford and Miss Fane.

'The engagement is announced between Basil Rainford, FRCS, eldest son of Colonel and Mrs Rainford, of Government House, Rawalpindi, India, and Hilary, only daughter of Professor James Fane, MA, LLD, and Mrs Fane, University Close, Edinburgh.'

ST CHRISTOPHER'S HOSPITAL

August 31st

Telephone messages

For Mr Rainford

Taken by Porter

Miss Fane wishing to say that she has decided in favour of flying scotsman leaving waverley stn ten am to-morrow can Mr Rainford come to station if not she will be in all evening packing furiously.

H MUNROE (Porter – W Door)

To Porter

Ring up Miss Fane (Univ 309) to say Mr Rainford at present in theatre, regrets he has a hysterotomy at eight o'clock to-night. Will do what he can to be at station to-morrow.

B R

Mrs Fane to Lady Barnley

UNIVERSITY CLOSE
EDINBURGH

August 31st

MY DEAR BERTHA,

How good of you to wire congratulations as soon as you heard! And of course I understand how my letter has only just reached you at Pau. It's always the same on holiday – one's correspondence so persistently follows one about.

But it *is* nice, isn't it? Have you met Basil? He's a remarkable young man, with a big career in front of him, James says. James has an immense respect for his brains – I don't feel that I really know him yet.

They're not to be married for a year. I don't approve of long engagements, but in this case Basil's work makes one necessary, and Hilary is determined not to spend the time at home doing nothing. Of course we'd love to have her – but you know how things are just now. I never realised before how many of James's offices were honorary! The child says that she won't have us scraping to give her an allowance. It's most unfortunate that the Library here couldn't keep her on. But one knows that they're hard hit too. Her present idea is to go to London with money for a month, and look for a temporary job there. I've made no objections – I'm sure the change will do her good – but of course I'm privately hoping that we shall have her back again by Christmas. She's going to the Minerva Hotel, which you always recommend. Mary Finnegan and the Bardsleys used to stay there, you remember. It's home like, as I told her, and quiet. Mercifully we managed to persuade her against unknown, cheap lodgings.

James sends his love, and would have added a note, but he is quite overwhelmed by his proofs of the last book on pre-Hellenic Greece at the moment. The study hasn't been touched by brush or duster for six weeks. You may just be thankful that Tom is a business man and safely out of the house in the mornings!

With best wishes to you both,

Your affectionate sister-in-law,

MARGARET FANE

Telegram

September 1st

Fane university close Edinburgh

Safely established at Minerva lots of letters follow

love,

HILARY

PART I – AUTUMN

MINERVA HOTEL
BEDDINGTON SQUARE
W2

September 1st

BASIL DEAR,

I've arrived, and the country post goes in five minutes. I don't like this hotel much. My bedroom is hung round with miniatory notices:

> NO WASHING OR DRYING OF GARMENTS MAY BE DONE IN THE BEDROOMS
>
> GUESTS ARE REQUESTED TO OBSERVE ECONOMY IN THE USE OF ELECTRIC LIGHT.
>
> ONE DAY'S NOTICE MUST BE GIVEN BEFORE LEAVING: OTHERWISE ROOMS WILL BE CHARGED FOR.

Their cumulative effect is shattering. Write me a long letter, not too obstetric.

Good-night: bless you,

HILARY

MINERVA HOTEL
BEDDINGTON SQUARE
W2

September 2nd

To: –
The Advertiser
Box 3141
Daily Post

SIR,

In reply to your advertisement of to-day's date offering a 'Lucrative Position to a Woman of Personality', I beg to apply for the post in question.

I am twenty-seven years of age, educated at Homedean School and Lady Hilda's College, Oxford, where I obtained an Honours Degree (Class II) in History.

For three years I was Assistant History Mistress at Glengyle High School for Girls, near Glasgow, and since then I have had considerable and varied secretarial experience. I have also acted as one of the Librarians at the Municipal Library, Corstorphine, Edinburgh. This post I held for two years, and left it solely because recent conditions necessitated a reduction in staff.

You do not state what qualifications are required, but I am confident that my general training would enable me to acquire any special knowledge easily and quickly. I am capable of taking responsibility and anxious for it.

I shall appreciate the favour of a personal interview at your convenience. Further particulars as to salary, hours, and nature of the employment offered would be welcome.

Yours faithfully,

HILARY FANE

PART I – AUTUMN

THE MINERVA

September 5th

MY DEAREST FAMILY,

I've been too busy for a mid-week letter, but I hope you liked the Houses of Parliament. The Minerva doesn't print postcards of itself, or I'd have put the proverbial cross below my window. Not that I've been there much: I've been chasing jobs, and heard of several, though I haven't actually got one yet.

Two interviews with possible employers are pending, though, and I do think that's encouraging, don't you? It's not as if I were hard to please. Almost any interesting job would do for a year. At about four pounds a week, I thought. After all, I'm not proposing to make a life-work of it.

I promise, though, that I won't hunt indefinitely. If nothing materialises you'll have me back in six weeks. (Don't count on that, of course, with two interviews to-morrow.)

Which shall I be, Confidential Secretary to a Psycho-therapeutist, or a Woman of Personality in a Business Concern? Both seem to think that I may be just the woman for them, and both use extremely impressive notepaper. And both promise Substantial Remuneration to the Right Personality.

On the whole, I think that the Business Concern would be best. The Psycho-therapeutist might clamour for shorthand, which would be so difficult. One may bluff about most qualifications, but one just either knows shorthand or not. And in my case not.

Good-night, my dears. I'll try to write fairly often once things settle down. In the meantime don't mind if my letters just let you know that I'm well and happy.

HILARY

PART I – AUTUMN

MINERVA

September 6th

From which you'll gather, darling, that I've retired to bed. I do understand now why it is that the Unemployed need to rest so much in the intervals of Genuinely seeking Work. It's just terribly exhausting. I've tried everything, from the grander kind of Advisory Bureau which caters for the University Woman to the Advertisements in the daily press and the Labour Exchange. No results so far.

I used to think that I'd a qualification or two: (they paid me rather heavily to teach History to the daughters of gentlemen.) But now, I doubt it. I started out, all buoyed up, for the Advisory place. They instantly charged me a fee, and then said that if I had capital to invest in training as a Decorator, Nurse, Window-dresser or Masseuse, they would be pleased to help me. So then I pointed out that I expected people to pay *me*. They gave me one look and said: 'In that case we don't think you've much chance. Still, you might try the Labour Exchange.'

Words passed. I began to think that a few pennyworth of stamps would be cheaper than expert advice. And said so. And swep' out. I went home, with the *Daily Post* – our paper – while my rage was still on me, and turned to the Situations Vacant. There were several exciting offers which began: 'Lucrative Position for Woman of Personality', and I felt sure that there couldn't be enough Women of Personality to go round them all. And wrote to ten, as impressively as possible. You remember that bit of typing I did for you in the summer? It may surprise you to know that it figures as 'considerable and varied secretarial experience!' So far only two of the advertisers have taken any notice. And to-day I went to interview them both.

Not a success, Basil, either of those interviews. I sat at the end of the first queue for an hour; then I was shown into a split-new office, where a beautiful and surprisingly cordial young man greeted me and offered a buoyant arm-chair. I sat into it, and he began to talk about Personality, Opportunity, and Ideals in Business. He went on for a long time, with suitable gesture, and I could neither get away nor bring him to the point.

Eventually it proved to be Corsets. It was further conveyed to me that I was expected to put down thirty pounds – what with one thing and what with another – for the privilege of selling them. The serpent said that it was a mere nothing 'compared to the profits'. And he seemed to think that I'd have quite a success with the Stout Gents' Belting. I don't doubt it, but I feel that with your prejudice against women in business you could hardly be expected to welcome the idea of *me* in Gents' Corsetry.

So I explained that I had neither thirty pounds nor a kind friend who would give or lend it, pawnable property nor sufficient faith to enter upon his sort of commercial venture. If his firm wanted me they could pay me to come to them. He dismissed me with evident nausea and sent for the dim spinster who had been before me in the queue.

I went on to my next interview a little dashed. This time it was with a purveyor of Psycho-therapy. He had a perfectly normal (female) secretary, so that I wasn't prepared to find him in a Biblical bath-robe, contemplating eternity in front of a Grecian vase with one lovely flower in it. I can't think what my duties would have been, but the word 'salary' shocked him nearly as much as the Corset gentleman. He murmured (in one of those organ voices) that he could not EMPLOY anyone untrained, though for a consideration he might allow me to serve him. After an exchange of banalities we parted – again, my dear Basil, quite largely because of my dutiful feelings towards you.

I made one more effort. I called on the Ever Ready Helpers. Have you heard of them?

> Got a problem? We'll solve it!
>
> Need help?   We'll give it!
>
> Got a talent? We'll use it!
>
> Lonely?   We'll find your twin soul!

So marvellous, don't you think? I paid half a crown for the privilege of laying my talents before them; but when they found that I didn't 'adore children' and wouldn't go and be a Mother's Help in the country they rather lost interest. I said something about being a secretary-chauffeuse, and they said: 'Oh, a secretary-chauffeuse … Yes. But we're afraid you're not the type.'

Finally, I went to the Labour Exchange. I felt that they at least might know of jobs with salaries attached and guaranteed respectable. Nobody'd call that place attractive, by the way. It's one of those unpleasant, dark-brown rooms with hard chairs and clerks with colds: the walls are hung with curling, dirty notices, all about Life in the Colonies, and a framed copy of the GFS Words to Girls Travelling. About half a dozen of us were waiting: different ages, shapes and sizes but all depressed. It was rather like the Out patients at Christophers – but undisinfected.

We waited ... for Hours. I was the last. When I was brought up before the Powers – two thin women – they asked me what kind of a job I wanted. I said: 'Oh, almost anything', and they cheered up. But when they found that I wasn't a cook they were terribly short with me. I asked if there weren't any other sort of places, and they looked me up and down and said darkly that it all depended. They had placed twenty people from Wales last week, but I was more difficult. (I hadn't the courage to ask why.) At last somebody had an idea. They suggested that I might be a Good Saleswoman. And what about a Bookshop? A degree, they said, would matter less there. It might almost cease to be a disadvantage.

Anyway, there are two definite openings! Messrs Brown's Universal Bookshop requires young ladies for their library, and there is another vacancy in Everyman's Stores. I've applied for both.

What sent my temperature rocketing up I don't know; but the main thing is to get it down in case either of them wants me. I've spent to-day recuperating, and it has stretched out beyond all recognition. I've slept a little, and read a little, and the hotel people have grudgingly brought up meals and clattered them down on my knees. Dreary meals, but possibly sustaining.

To think that it's less than a week since I left you, and that you didn't want me to go and I might have stayed ... Only, I know I couldn't wait for you if I were idle, sitting about and trying to fill the gap between one lovely experience and another with those dreary little sociabilities that you despise as much as I do. I wish I had the kind of talents that you'd really like to have about the house, my lamb. It would all be so much simpler if my bent were music or if I could write. But it isn't any use, Basil, I haven't any talents; even my drawing's always got me into trouble. I've just got undecorative ability and too much energy to be happy without a job.

But – oh, dear!

H

MINERVA HOTEL
BEDDINGTON SQUARE
W2

September 9th, 1931

To: –
The Staff Supervisor
Everyman's Stores
Oxford Street
W1

MADAM,

The Labour Exchange, Great Yarmouth Street, has informed me that you require an assistant in one of your departments, and I therefore venture to apply for the post, enclosing their introduction.

I am twenty-seven years of age, and have had some secretarial experience. During the past two years I have been employed in the Municipal Library, Corstorphine, Edinburgh, but a reduction in staff has made it necessary for me to leave.

I should be most grateful if you would consider my application: if you wish to see me, I can come for an interview at any time.

Should you require testimonials I will send them, and I enclose a stamped and addressed envelope for a reply to this application at your convenience.

Yours faithfully,
HILARY FANE

PART I – AUTUMN

EVERYMAN'S STORES

OXFORD STREET

W1

'Our business is your pleasure.'

September 10th, 1931

The Staff Supervisor will be glad if you will come and see her at the above address to-morrow morning at eleven o'clock.

        (Signed)
        M E WARD
        STAFF SUPERVISOR

MISS HILARY FANE
MINERVA HOTEL
BEDDINGTON SQUARE
W2

BT/MEW

Telegram

September 11th

Fane university close Edinburgh.

Got a job details follow.

HILARY

PART I – AUTUMN

THE MINERVA

Friday evening
September 11th

BASIL DEAR,

I meant to write to you last night, but I waited, because I thought there might be a letter. And there was – a very sweet one. Bless you! But I don't think one enjoys: 'I told you so' however beautifully it's put. It isn't true, either. I'VE GOT A JOB. So I won't be coming to heel just yet.

All the same, to be quite honest, I'm not so very pleased. I'd set my heart on the bookshop. It's nearer my own line. But they wouldn't have me. They said I was too tall; certainly all the people I saw to-ing and fro-ing were neat little creatures. The officials were gentle and kind, but utterly unencouraging: I didn't venture to mention the word 'waiting-list'. Besides, I'm not really prepared to wait.

So I went on to Everyman's, more or less as to my last hope. And it materialised, Basil, into an offer of work, immediate, whole-time, salaried work. For that I'm thankful. For the rest – well, one can't judge yet.

I began wrong, of course. I went in at the main entrance, and one of those large, buttoned men they keep loomed up at me and asked if he 'might help, Madam?'

I said: 'Well, I've got an appointment with the Staff Supervisor', and I think that his face went through the funniest transformation I've ever seen in my life. There was a sort of convulsion, and when it was over all the deference had gone. However, he did indicate a door with a curtain over it, and told me that if I went that way no doubt I should find someone to direct me. I got as far as the Supervisor's room and then had another of those waits outside it, on a hard chair in a draughty passage. Finally I was summoned, and left alone with a large lady, very well girthed, in a room full of weighing-machines and card-indexes. I stood meekly till she asked me to sit down, and began a series of questions, none of which seemed relevant. I kept my degree dark for quite a long time, but it shocked her less than I expected when I finally owned to it. She said, yes, they did take on some graduates now and then, but only as an experiment, of course. Titles were better value, I gathered.

Then she discovered that I'd done librarian's work as well as teaching. That seemed to interest her, and she asked so many more questions that I thought a really exciting job might be forthcoming. It wasn't. She ended the catechism by asking if

'A LARGE LADY, VERY WELL GIRTHED.'

I 'liked gels'. I said that I didn't, but that I could cope with them, and she told me blandly that if I realised how dull the work would be, and if, in spite of that, I really wanted the post, she could offer me £2:10:0 a week. So I goggled, but kept my head sufficiently to ask what exactly the work would be. She went vague at that, like everybody else, but said that perhaps I would do better on the Book Floor than in the Millinery, where they were also shorthanded. I thought that sounded likely and said so, and she explained that I should probably not be in the selling department at all, of course, but somewhere behind the scenes. As a clerk. Somebody insignificant developed appendicitis last night, it seems. That's why they're taking me on.

A clerk: it sounds dreary, but I daren't refuse. It may lead to something, after all. (I wonder how many people get themselves landed for incredible years by that hope and by being too scared afterwards to throw up one job and look for another?) Anyway, I took it. I may have been a fool. I know there's precious little prospect of advancement unless one's head and shoulders better than the other people. But if I am, and if someone who matters notices it in time, I shall have my chance.

Only, you can see why I'm not jubilant.

Tell me about yourself. I expect you're hideously busy now you're back from that shooting party. I must say I was hurt when never a bird reached London, though, as you very properly pointed out, I wouldn't have known what to do with game in a hotel.

Is your assistant to be long away? I'm afraid you won't have much chance of getting on with your book for a while. Or does difficulty wake the same devil in you as it does in me, I wonder. (I don't mean that for virtue. Rather the contrary.)

Something cussed makes me lie flat on my back and purr when things go well. My sort of weakling can only get things done under opposition, I suppose. And that's partly why I'm taking on this job, my lamb.

They want me to begin on Monday: I must go to bed now. Good-night: I love you.

HILARY

PS – How long does it take to have appendicitis? Comfortably, I mean.

From the Official Records of Messrs Everyman & Co

APPLICATION FOR EMPLOYMENT

Name (in full)	Hilary Ervine Fane,
Present Address	Minerva Hotel, Beddington Sq, W2
Permanent Address	University Close, Edinburgh
Age	Twenty-seven
Nationality	Scots
Denomination	
Last Employment	Assistant Librarian
Department	Municipal Library, Corstorphine, Edinburgh

Cause and Date of Leaving   Reductions in Staff. May 1931.

Qualifications   B.A. (Hons) Oxon. Three years teaching; two years librarian work. Typing. French and German.

I, the undersigned, declare that these facts are, to the best of my knowledge, correct, and I agree to the following terms on which employment with Everyman's Stores Limited, depends: –

Salary £2:10:0 per week   *Hours* 9-6

Date of commencing Work Monday, September 14th, 1931

Employment may be terminated by one week's notice from either party. In the event of any misdemeanour, this notice may be waived by the Company.

                    (Signed)   Hilary Ervine Fane

Health and Unemployment cards must be handed to the Cashier on beginning work. Failure to do this involves a fine.

MINERVA HOTEL

September 12th

DEAREST MUMMY AND DADDY,

Yes, it is rather a comfort, isn't it? I'm glad that you thought the occasion called for a telegram in reply to mine. I have a suspicion, though, that you were subterraneously sad as well as pleased. I know what a lovely welcome you'd have given the prodigal if London hadn't wanted her. And during the last week I'll admit that I thought London was going to have nothing to do with me at all.

Jobs aren't as easy to find as they seemed: most of the ones I investigated weren't suitable. So I've had to take what I could get, as everyone else is doing. Probably, of course, it'll lead to something more exciting. Its beginnings don't sound much. I've been offered a clerical job in Messrs Everyman's big store in Oxford Street. You know it – the *Our Business is your Pleasure* people. Aunt Bertha used to send us their catalogues and a few rather remnantish presents now and then when Uncle Tom was first made president of that Amalgamated Board, you remember. I don't quite know the connection, but there is an almost directorial one, I believe.

I'm to begin at once. Somebody has thoughtfully got appendicitis and I'm deputising. So of course I mean to make myself essential enough to be kept on when she recovers. I was only interviewed by one official who appointed me, and I don't know anything about the work except that I'm to be attached to the Book Floor, which is pleasant. (Think of me in the Haberdashery, trying to add up one-and-eleven-threes!) I'll be able to tell you more on Monday. It's going to be very amusing, I expect. And after all, isn't half the English aristocracy earning its living by selling hats or displaying gowns or making facecreams or breeding dogs or foxes or poultry or ponies? So don't be disappointed. Basil won't really mind, either, you know, though of course he felt he had to protest. It was only becoming.

And after all, dears, a year can't reasonably last longer than twelve months, and in a year I shall come home and be unobtrusively married. Then we'll be more or less on your doorstep. It isn't as if Basil were apt to go off and grow cotton in the Sudan or plant tea in India. He's only going to operate in Edinburgh, and once housekeeping worries begin you'll be liable to have more than enough of me. I shall annex your recipes and harry you with questions about servants' wages and leaving cards and sending out invitations and seating people at dinner, and washing curtains and making marmalade. And we'll borrow Anderson to wait on our statelier parties.

So make the most of this year's grace!

> Very much love,
>
> **HILARY**

BUSINESS AS USUAL

EVERYMAN'S STORES

For use in inter-departmental correspondence only.

From Staff Supervisor   *To* Miss Hopper C/D
                                   Book Floor

                                   September 12th

Subject Temporary Staff. Clerical Department B/F

Memo

I have arranged for a new assistant to take over Miss Pim's duties during her absence (appendicitis). Miss Fane will report to you on Monday morning at nine o'clock in the Clerical Department. She has had no previous experience of this type of work, and it will therefore be necessary to train her most carefully in all the details of departmental routine.

MEW

BI/MEW

PART I – AUTUMN

THE MINERVA

September 14th

Oh, Basil darling, I suppose there have only been the usual number of hours since eight o'clock this morning. But it's hard to believe. I had breakfast then, in the empty dining-room. A depressed maid brought it and she seemed undecided whether to sympathise or to despise me, because I had to be up almost as early as she did. I left the hotel in a flutter and before they'd finished the doorsteps.

Of course I was too early. After ten minutes in a bus quite indecently full of human knees and elbows we turned into Oxford Street, where Everyman's big clock said only twenty minutes to nine. So I got out and wandered up the mews to the Staff Entrance. No swing doors for us of course.

MEMBERS OF THE STAFF MUST ENTER AND LEAVE THE BUILDING BY THE STAFF DOOR. THEY ARE FORBIDDEN TO USE THE FRONT ENTRANCE (OR THE LIFTS).

The Staff Door is in Manifold Lane. I knew where that was, because I went prospecting on Sunday and liked it too much to regret the commissionaires. Manifold Lane must be one of the villages that were swallowed up alive by London in the eighteenth century, and managed to go on living. Very cramped, of course. Like Jonah in the whale.

So this morning I had time to enjoy the last ten minutes of being unemployed. I looked at people as one does on the way to the dentist, envying them because their morning was going to be smooth and usual. The Lane's a cheery place, paved with a gentle tilt towards the gutter in the middle. The crumbling little shops sell a muddle of antiques and cigarettes and chocolates and Italian cheeses and German sausages and jellied eels and jumpers and spectacles and stationery and walking-sticks and toupees and face powders. There's a flower shop at one end and a fish shop in the middle. The fish man had laid out his herrings and lobsters, and eels in patterns and he was festooning poor limp rabbits round the windows as I came past. Then he backed across the gutter with his head on one side. Like an artist at a Private View.

But at the Everyman's end of the Lane the flags change to cobbles and the elderly shops to hustling garages. Big, bright blue vans with EVERYTHING FROM EVERYMAN'S placarded up on their roofs like cocks' combs were sliding out and backing up, and having parcels shot into them by men in shirt-sleeves. I stood and watched, till a sort of fire-alarm thing above the Staff Entrance went off and made me jump like Cinderella. It's not merely nine to six for inmates of Stores like Everyman's, you see. We clock in at ten to nine and out at ten past six, they tell me. *Streams* of people were making for the Staff Entrance: I was nearly at the end of a very slow-moving line. I couldn't imagine why it was so slow till I got inside; then I saw a row of large dials like telephone automatic things in a nightmare. They were as big as cart-wheels and there were hundreds of white discs round the rims of each, with red and black numbers on them. People came up and pushed their special number in. Apparently the abominable thing records the hour, the minute and the second on which everyone enters that building on three hundred and however many working days there are a year.

I couldn't clock in, because I hadn't got a number. So the man in charge kept me back on suspicion. I stood beside him in his cubby-hole while the rather breathless people at the tail of the queue came up. They all eyed me: it reminded me of the time I was knocked out in a car smash and found myself on the pavement with a crowd round me. Rather terrifying. A sort of jungle look. I tried to forget them and listen to the timekeeper's running commentary instead. He was a cheerful person, without much to do except look out for numberless creatures like me, and prevent other people from dialling their best friends' numbers while they took a day off. He sat just outside the notice at the end of the passage which promised that ANY MEMBER OF THE STAFF FOUND SMOKING BEYOND THIS NOTICE WILL BE INSTANTLY DISMISSED, with a cigarette rolling on his lower lip. He had tilted his kitchen chair on to its hind-legs:

'Now then, Miss Brown ... never a smile to-day? Get out of the wrong side of the bed Monday mornings, eh? ... Half a minute to spare, Mr Henry? That train's been up to time at London Bridge for once! ... Better weather over the week-end, Mr Willis...And how's the old complaint, Alfred? ... Back to the grindstone, Miss Anderson ... that's right. Shame, isn't it, for that pretty nose? ...'

When the last had gone through he swung his chair round and asked me what he could do to oblige. So I told him that I'd come to work, and waited while he thumbed and licked his way through a pile of elderly papers. He rang up one or two people on the telephone beside his chair, shouted up the stairs to a Mr Hardway on the floor above who either didn't hear or didn't answer, and then went off down the passage grumbling to find someone who knew something about me. Presently he came back. 'OK, Miss. You'll be all right to-morrow. Your number'll come through by this evening or should do.'

I'd always thought that it must be utterly dreadful to be just a number. But you try not having a number at all, and to all intents and purposes no name either. It's an incredibly left-out-at-Creation feeling. Next morning, I thought, I should be able to stare at the numberless with the rest of the herd.

It is an amazing place, Basil. Stairs and stairs. As a customer one used to sail into a lift and say 'Fifth, please', without a notion of what's involved for the people who walk. We climbed and climbed. Conversation faltered after we'd passed the third floor, and I caught up the tail at the fourth, where it had died altogether.

Six floors up we seethed through a door marked CLOAKROOM WOMEN STAFF, and into a large unpleasant room. It was pinkly distempered and tapestried with people's coats and hats. I suppose there had been pegs, but they were submerged. I laid my coat on the floor and wondered what came next. But a forbidding person in uniform came up and pointed at it. 'Pick it up,' she said. 'Catching the dust like that. Most unhealthy.'

And she went on to explain that the cloakroom was provided for people working in the Departments. Who was I, her tone suggested, a mere cipherless newcomer, to walk in and expect pegs all ready for me? I gathered that I would be lucky if I were allowed occasionally to turn a wash-basin tap, tip one of the soap vases, provided by Messrs Jeevers & Co as an advertisement, and to stand in a queue during the less busy hours. (Life, my dear, seems now likely to resolve itself into a series of those queues. And I'm so *bad* at them.)

Who *was* I, anyway, said the blue-uniformed person? She, for her part, was Sister Smith, and responsible for the health of the Female Staff. (So Biblical, that classification! Is there a Brother to look after the health of the males in their cloakroom?) I explained. I had come for the first time. I had no number, but I believed that I was to go to the Clerical Department on the Book Floor. It seemed that there had been a culpable oversight on the part of Somebody. I, as a newcomer, ought never to have been allowed to set foot in that building until I had been examined by Sister Smith. 'It's too late now, of course,' she told me. 'You may have brought in anything with you. *Anything.*'

Then she said quite kindly that of course it was mere formality when all was said and done, but that I'd better come to her room at eleven and she would see to it. In the meantime she found a peg for me behind the door and took me to the Clerical Department of the Book Floor, one flight down. When we arrived Sister Smith called through a blinding racket of typewriters for 'Mr Simpson, please'. The women all raised their heads and gave me another of those jungle looks, but the racket went on as fast as ever. That glimpse of expert typing terrified me: I have to keep my eyes glued on my keys throughout.

Then Mr Simpson came round a wall of books. He's a large, baldish, undefined sort of person, who moved, but vaguely. Rather like a cloud. None of his clothes fit him: his knees sag in shiny striped trousers. But he smiled at me and I smiled back thankfully. He said:

'So you've come to help us, Miss. That'll be nice.'

There was a pause. Sister Smith, who presumably has no patience with pauses, said: 'Well, there you are then.' And went off, clapping the door behind her. Mr Simpson stood and watched it swing for a little, then looked at me uncertainly. He tried again:

'You're to work for Miss Hopper, Miss, so they tell me. She's over there.' He pointed somewhere behind me. 'That's her table. She'll be back in a minute, I expect.'

I walked between books and typewriters to Miss Hopper's table, slowly, because it was something definite to do, and after I'd done it I didn't know what to do next. When I got there, I just stood, like a cow looking over a gate, and waited for something to happen.

It's odd: the things that aren't alive in that Clerical Room – typewriters and chairs and filing cupboards – seem much more vital than the people, who are. I noticed the books next. There were masses of them: all colours, reds and greens and blues and oranges. They were in baskets, in gaping parcels, in tottering piles on tables, each with a pinkish slip of paper sticking out, like a tired dog's tongue. (Customers' names and addresses, I found out later.) More books were ranged round the room, looking normal because they were on shelves.

At last someone came. I guessed it was Miss Hopper, because she said she'd been expecting me. She was a sagging sort of person with short, just greying hair. Wearing red. She opened one of the table drawers and dragged out a checked duster. 'I suppose you'd better get on,' she said. 'My last girl used to have done dusting by now.'

I said: 'Oh. What do I dust?' And Miss Hopper supposed it was the table. So I took up the checked duster while she stood lop-sidedly on, one leg and watched me. After a few minutes she supposed I'd been used to keeping my place tidy at my last job. Of course *she'd* always had a girl. Her other girl had been ever so neat and filled the ink-pots every morning. But just at that point I knocked one over, and as I clawed at the blotting-paper some of the books went too. Miss Hopper said: 'Oh, dear, miss, that's a pity, isn't it?' and went on watching while I mopped and picked up. By that time it was, incredibly, only ten o'clock, but Miss Hopper supposed again that we'd better get on.

She sat down and asked me if I was a good writer. I looked at the stacked books and said hastily that I didn't write at all. But Miss Hopper was so utterly taken aback that I gathered that she meant could I use a pen so that the result would be legible on labels. That shook me, but I said that I could print quite neatly, I thought. It seemed that that would do, though postmen wouldn't enjoy it so much.

After that Miss Hopper produced the labels. They were a quite unreasonably unpleasant pink, with dotted lines for the addresses. Books appeared too, clamped together in twos and threes by rubber bands. Sometimes there were ten books inside the band and then it generally snapped in my face when I tried to push a label inside. 'Why *didn't* you take that band off first?' said Miss Hopper each time it happened.

I wrote labels till eleven, with interruptions from people called Packers, who seemed short-tempered. At least they brought back several of my labels and pointed out that I had forgotten part of the address. At eleven o'clock someone telephoned to say that Miss Fane was to go to Sister's room at once. Miss Hopper said: 'You can't miss it', but Mr Simpson wandered up and pointed out the way.

Both the windows in Sister's room were open. So was the door (opposite) and I stood in the draught, wondering how much I should have to undress. Sister Smith said: 'Shut the door. Take off your shoes. Stand on that weighing machine. Left foot first.'

Then she pulled a sort of medical catechism out of a pigeon-hole in her bureau and read out the questions while I dithered on my perch. They began with 'state of head' and worked intimately downwards. Finally Sister looked at the weights, and said, 'Nine stone ten. Your feet aren't flat – yet. Step off. Right foot.'

I shuffled into my shoes while she asked me if both parents were alive and did I suffer from nerves. I said: 'Yes. Church of Scotland. I don't know what nerves are.'

Sister told me severely that denomination was a matter for the individual conscience, but that nerves were not. They might affect the Firm. And she did hope that I hadn't the habit of taking a morning in bed now and then. Because once a thing like that crept in among the people who ought to know better what was one to do with the junior typists?

Then she sent me back to the Clerical Department, and I went, wondering how long it would be before my feet flattened. I shall have to leave before then. I've heard your views on flat-footed women.

After that I wrote more labels, till they let me out at half-past twelve. I suppose I went and ate something somewhere, but when I came back again afterwards, Miss Hopper said that she didn't want me any more that afternoon, and I'd better go and ask Miss Sparling in the Library if she had any letters. That was, if I could type. Could I? I remembered the women who had beaten the typewriters when I came in and hesitated to own to my two-fingered champings. But with my sort of horror of being flung out I had to say I could.

'That's right,' said Miss Hopper. 'Well, you'd better go to Miss Sparling. Take that door opposite (but mind you shut it behind you. It's the Shop out there, and customers aren't supposed to see the Clerical Department.) Go through the Shop and if you turn to the right through the swing doors you're in the Library. Miss Sparling's the lady at the big desk.'

The Shop (that seems to be the local name for the selling department of the Book Floor) was interesting. Books were in their element there, praised and ranked and jacketed, handled respectfully by a polite young man and six polite, sleek little girls who ran about among the well-dressed customers with dogs on leads.

I would have liked to stay and look at things, but I was feeling intimidated, so I went straight through to the Library, which is a long, busy room with ticketed shelves and people reading in corners. It was quite easy to find Miss Sparling. She had the biggest desk, and was bristling behind the vase of semi-putrid Michaelmas daisies which stood on it. She had a nasty, pointed, rattish face. When I said: 'Miss Hopper sent me from the Clerical Department to see if you could make any use of me,' she lifted her nose at me quite malevolently. 'Make use of you? No.' And she picked up another pile of papers and fussed it from one side of her desk to the other, as if I'd disappeared through the earth. And I'm sure I was quite meek.

So I went back to the Clerical Department, thinking, in my innocence, that they might send me home as they'd no work for me. But they didn't: work at that level means primarily being on and about the premises for a certain number of hours to take what people put on you. That's what they pay us for. And finally, I was given something to do. They made me write things on little buff cards till six o'clock. Then Mr Simpson roused me and explained that it was all over.

Darling, don't scold me for taking this on. It's hard, but it may improve. I'm too dazed just at present to judge its points. And such lots of people would jump at it. They wouldn't even think it hard. It's all so relative.

I met a woman in the bus this evening who was teaching with me at Glengyle. She went on to a big advisory post with a firm in Nottingham – she had a First-class degree in Science – a brilliant woman. But they've cut down their staff too, and she's been workless for six months, so desperate that she seriously considered trying the corset job that I turned down. She's thirty-seven, of course, not twenty-seven. I can fail and start again. And with you to believe in my work, I could.

Only, now and then, I feel you don't. Do try to. I mean, think of me as a *creature*, not just as a possible wife who will persist in doing things that tend to disqualify her. I love you frightfully; but I want your companionship and tolerance and understanding even more than other things. I wonder if you see?

Good-night, my dear,

HILARY

PS – This is an incredibly long letter: all about Me.

PPS – Still, it *is* funny, don't you think? Or don't you?

PART I – AUTUMN

THE MINERVA

September 15th

BASIL DEAR,

I was *very* glad to get your letter. It's good news that you think you can afford to run a car this year. I've always thought it would be worth while, in many ways. As you say, it'll mean getting to the golf course in a quarter of the usual time. It may sound absurd, but *I'm* still enjoying buses. I had to stand this morning all the way, because I didn't use my elbows as well as usual at Lancaster Gate. And I even liked swinging about and watching London from the knees down.

I admit that it'll wear off, but just at present I like seeing people scrambling for the Tube Stations and getting in the way of the other people trying to sweep doorstep dust into the gutters and sluice pavements and deliver milk and empty dustbins, and do all the things that are finished with and hushed up when the merely leisured come out of their houses at eleven o'clock.

I like the wet door-steps and polished doorknobs and piles of newspapers in sheltered corners, and shops with the shutters and grid things half-open and men with bowler hats ducking in and out, and girls in bedroom slippers putting last touches to window displays.

There seem to be so many more horses about at nine o'clock too. Lots of philosophic, chilly-looking men on drays refuse to be hurried, and to-day four carts were racing round Marble Arch in front of our bus. They'd come from Covent Garden and their drivers were waving whips and cursing cheerfully. A little man with a cartload of cabbages and a trotting donkey was behind them, taking up most of the fairway. Our conductor leant out, and shouted: 'Now then, Ben Hur, get off the rails!' And the donkey bolted.

Opposite Bond Street I get off and walk up Manifold Lane to the Staff Entrance. The Lane's busier than Oxford Street at this time of day. I've no idea that so many old women went to work on outside jobs: I met dozens of them, plodding about with string bags or queer parcels. I suppose they're chars, or dailies, coming from making other people's breakfasts; quite unresentfully, most of them, because they've done that sort of thing all their lives. And some still older women go from one dust-bin to another with sacks at this time of day: they lift the lids and finger the muddle inside with grey, careful hands that never miss a bottle or a crust.

'OLDER WOMEN GO FROM ONE DUST-BIN TO ANOTHER ...'

Half-way along the Lane I usually begin to run, hypnotised by that clock over the Staff Entrance. After that come the million stairs to the Cloakroom (Women Staff) so that I inevitably arrive on the Book Floor without a breath in my body. While dusting Hopper's premises my heart returns to normal and my face de-purples itself. I've begun to know the geography of the place now, so I'm less bewildered, though I don't know the people as well as I know the places where they work, on the whole. They still tend to be rather cardboard, except Miss Sparling, who's something much more malignant, and Mr Simpson, who's like a wax figure on a warm day instead. In an emergency he'd be liable to melt altogether. He's continually bullied by Mr Millet, whose efficiency is almost indecent. I suspect Mr Millett of being one of those magnates in the making. Five years ago he was riding an errand bicycle (with his hands in his pockets instead of on the handle-bars, I expect) and twenty-five years hence he may be writing his memoirs. In the meantime he treats me kindly and Shows me the Ropes.

Talking of magnates, there's one called Grant who runs the firm's publicity and seems to be making himself generally felt throughout the building. I gather from Hopper that his visits to the Book Floor are cyclonic. She was reverential about his new circular introducing our Rational Reading Service; but I brought one home in case I got depressed. It's all about his latest library system. Books are to be delivered to subscribers daily at the same time as groceries, shoes, silk underwear, model gowns, or whatever those subscribers have bought at Everyman's. You see the idea? One department helps another, and the blue vans deliver the lot.

And, incidentally, every blue van carries a new placard these days. Most sensational:

> Bread for the basket?
>
> Yes!
>
> Books for the brain?
>
> Everyman's bring them
>
> And
>
> Change them again!

I can foresee some truly marvellous complications. His circular buttonholes the British public:

> We know your trouble. You never have a minute. Yet you love to read. And you are right. Good reading is as essential as good living. But in the fret and fume of modern life how are you to find time to choose, from the multitude of books published every day, yes,

almost every hour, the best for your reading? For it must be the best. We know that. May we not help you? Everyman's will provide your mental food as well as your daily stores. We will send novels with your groceries, biographies with your butcher-meat, plays with your fruit. More. They will be the *best*. They will be chosen for you, with special reference to your individual and entirely personal taste and views on literature, by our cultured, experienced librarians, whose fingers are ever on the pulse of modern literature.

'That's me,' said Hopper, breathing proudly down my neck. I told her that I thought it was lovely, but what I wanted to know most was whether this man Grant has a really reliable sense of humour or just a very earnest, high-powered commercial mind. What did she think?

She looked rather staggered at that heretical problem, and said that she'd never really thought about it at all, but surely I never thought the circular funny, did I? I changed the subject, and asked her if she chose all the books. She said yes, she did. And Miss Sparling too, of course. It was ever so interesting. I should be able to help her a little, perhaps, when she'd trained me. But until I'd mastered the routine of the business she couldn't expect me to be much use to her, of course.

Then I asked her how long she thought it would take me to learn, and she supposed that all depended. But it seems to be a question of years, if not decades. By the look she gave my last batch of labels, I'm afraid she favours the decades. Still, she said that I might begin to learn the card-indexing system in a day or two, if I didn't get behind with my labels. So I started in at once. After two hours my wrist ached till I thought it would be better if it *did* drop off, but Hopper counted my labels in a surprised way and promised to show me the card-index tomorrow. Largely, I think, to keep me quiet. I'm afraid she finds me turbulent: too many things upset in my vicinity.

To-night I walked home across the Park. It was very pleasant; a clear sky with the beginnings of frost. I went very fast, and by the time I got to Beddington Square I was hot and tired, and muddled with mental arithmetic.

Because, if I could walk home every day and get up a little earlier in the mornings to walk to work I should save fourpence a day. And, taking four days a week – in case it rained once or twice – that would be one and fourpence saved in a week. And five and fourpence a month. Quite a lot can be done with five and fourpence: a Pit, a day in the country, a shampoo and set. No more buses.

But when I went upstairs to change I found a large, potato-shaped hole in each heel.

In favour of walking, twice daily for one month: . . 5/4

Against: one new pair of stockings daily: 5/11

That's how life gets you!

Love,

HILARY

LUNCH TIME

September 17th

WELL, DARLING,

I'm writing this in a teashop. It's called Green Corners, I suppose because the tables are painted an unpleasant pea-soup colour. No tablecloths. But one can get an eatable and filling lunch for 1/6. So I shall come here often. They leave you in your corner for long peaceful intervals. Soup ... meat ... sweet ... and /or coffee. Since I'm not in a hurry, it doesn't drive me mad. I bring a writing pad or a book, and watch people between whiles. I come a little late, to have the long half of the day behind me. Of course my inside is a protesting vacuum during the last hour. But it's worth it. I emerge, triumphant and ravenous, about half-past one.

More ravenous than triumphant to-day. It's been one of those grey mornings with the streets full of cripples. One's mind see-saws between pity for oneself and for all the people who walk lame or trundle barrel-organs or sit propped up against the railings of the Park with a row of decorated flagstones in front of them. Only a hundred yards of street between Everyman's Staff Entrance and the teashop, but by the time I'd reached Green Corners I could hardly bear life.

But the people who come here to lunch every day seem quite pleased with things. There are lots of young women in hip-length fur (or fur-like) coats from offices or the other big shops round about. I've never seen anybody from Everyman's here. I know that lots of them eat at the Canteen. But I didn't take kindly to the idea. 'All girls together ...' No thank you. So I race out and compete for the corner tables with the other people who set store by them. There's one little clerk who glares at me as if I'd done something mortal whenever I get to the window table before he does. And I glare back. But when he gets there first and I glare at him he filters his soup triumphantly through his moustache as if I weren't on the planet.

There are lots of unexplained people. I want to know about the two who have a table reserved for them every day. The woman always comes, but sometimes the man doesn't turn up. Then she waits half an hour and goes away again, without lunch. They're middle aged, and the man wears spats which shine among the wrinkling socks of Green Corners. They always have a great deal to say as if it were their only opportunity. And there are three spinsters with that look of calculated cheerfulness that's so dreadfully depressing. They come up from the country once a week or thereabouts and talk about what's happening to Mary ... and Beryl ... and Joan ... since she left school. There's one girl who comes occasionally, with a face like a Bellini Madonna and *Home Chat* under her arm.

I wonder where the men on the Book Floor lunch. On the one occasion I visited the Canteen very few males were there. Do they go to Lyons? Or to pubs? Or Dining Rooms? There are some steamy-windowed ones in Manifold Lane which have a fascination for me. I've not dared to investigate so far. Tell me about Dining Rooms: can a girl go there? Alone? Or should I have to persuade somebody to take me? I have a feeling that Mr Millett and Mr Salt lunch in a Dining Room. Certainly they go off together, looking odd. Mr Millett's education was County Council, Night School, and a day trip to Cambridge at Whitsun. So he wears grey flannel trousers and a brownish, hairy tweed coat and no hat in the street, because he knows that those are the things that count. And Mr Salt was a noise in the crowd at Trinity, so he wears a celluloid collar, bowler

'THEY GO OFF TOGETHER, LOOKING ODD.'

hat and striped trousers because he knows that *those* are the things that count. (Being in Rome …) I believe that they're great friends. But neither challenges the other's costume in spite of all the meals they eat together.

Yesterday Miss Dowland asked me to share her tea-table in the ABC. (More about meals, Basil. I always seem to be writing at them or about them. But they loom so, when you pay cash.) Anyway, I went to tea with Miss Dowland yesterday. The waitress asked her what she would take. She said:

'Well, I don't feel just like cake. I think I'll just have the tea, Mabel.' And the fat Mabel said:

'Oh, there now, you know you ought to. It keeps the strength up.'

Miss Dowland wavered.

'Perhaps I'll have a bun, after all.' But she looked at the cakes (twopence each) on the cutglass stand. I asked her if she usually came to that shop. She said: 'Yes. Fifteen years, off and on it'll be now.'

And she still counts the days. 'This is my seven-hundredth-and-fiftieth Monday,' she told me when I crawled upstairs at the beginning of this week. So she once expected something to happen. And in another twenty years or so something will. She'll collect her superannuation and her pension and retire. She has a house: 'So nice, Miss Fane, quite in the country. Out at Harrow. The air's so fresh, I always say.' She lives with her friend, who's been 'out' this last six months. 'We hope she'll get something – anything almost – soon. It's a little difficult for the two of us when only one's earning.' And I saw her look at my ring. I don't want to gloat, but I *am* glad about us, Basil.

Time's up. I'll post this on the way back.

>Love, always,
>
>**HILARY**

Bus

September 18th

Pay Day, my lamb. And I'm alive to claim it! No earnings have ever pleased me so much. And I'm fairly certain that the management have seldom spent a salary to less purpose.

To label-writing: two pounds ten. Well!

Goodness knows I'm neither deft nor diligent, and even you can't (always) read my writing.

But they paid me. In a little, thick, yellow envelope, with the flap so glued down that it defied even the most honest efforts to up-end it. The name of the department was stamped in bright blue letters; my own above was neatly printed in block caps. Inside were two pound notes, two half-crowns, three shillings, a sixpence and three coppers. By rights there should have been the two pounds ten they promised me, but Ill-health and Unemployment have to be considered. They *make* you contribute to these things. Did you know? I was told on my first day that I must get my Unemployment card at the Labour Exchange in some street or other whose name I instantly forgot, and the Health card at any Post Office. Can *you* ever find Post Offices at a crisis? I can't. But they subtract the one and threepence, just the same.

Anyway, the envelopes were brought round after tea by our Mr Simpson. His boots squeak, but his feet are beautiful on the mountains on those occasions, and he knows it. There is a sort of annunciatory expression on his flat face which is most suitable. I didn't know whether one thanked him with all the gratitude one felt or ignored the existence of anything which might give the lie to the WORK FOR WORK'S SAKE notice which hangs opposite Miss Sparling's desk in the Library. So I watched the others from my corner. No one said thank you;

so I didn't. Miss Lamb beamed: Miss Hopper pushed her envelope quickly into her bag; but Miss Watts sat back and counted every item with the lovely crackling tweak at the corners of her notes that I've envied bank cashiers all my life. There was a new, Friday evening sound in the Department; the semi-surreptitious counting of everybody's loose change, guardedly, so that other people mightn't see exactly what was going into each handbag or trousers pocket.

I'd hardly stowed away my share before Mr Sirnpson came up to me again, this time more or less on tip-toe, and asked me whether I would like to start paying in to the Superannuation Fund when I was eligible. That, of course, wouldn't be for six months yet. I thought it was a charity. But he explained, and it seems that whenever one has been six months in the firm one begins to save against the day when failing eyes, legs and ears force one to leave it. I hedged a little, and he told me that they all did it, even Miss Lamb. (And she's twenty.) So when he had assured me that I could get it back 'in the event of dismissal' (that seemed to be the only reason for leaving which occurred to him) I promised to contribute.

Later

Your letter came in by the last post and I thought I'd add a bit to mine before going to bed. I'm writing in dressing-gown and bedroom slippers, comforted by a bath rather more than by your lecture on morbidity. But I'll give your remarks my attention. I'm quite meek, you know. In essentials.

Perhaps my last letter *was* a bit full of pavement artists and indigent spinsters. And, as you say, they probably neither deserve nor want to be pitied. It doesn't hurt them (as people say when they kill moths). Of course they like crowds. Look at Blackpool. And work, because, as you say, they wouldn't know what to do with leisure if they had it. Though that does seem such a hoary and suspicious argument – or do I mean specious, by any chance? Of course, I know you're right up to a point. They're not unhappy. I was watching Miss Lamb this morning, during a beatific pause in the label-writing due to a failure in the supply of raw material. She was completely absorbed in typing her letter. She never wasted a second or made an unnecessary gesture whipping out one sheet and putting in another. There must be some satisfaction in doing anything, even if it's mechanical, quite as well as she does. And yet, there's nothing to show for all her work but her initials sandwiched with those of her principal in the bottom left-hand corner of hundreds, thousands, and perhaps, in twenty years, millions of letters. Which is probably a very sour-grapeish remark. I couldn't turn out Miss Lamb's faultlessly typed pages if I tried all my life.

But Miss Lamb doesn't mean to spend a lifetime on hers. She was talking to me about the Future in the cloakroom queue before lunch today. She's got permission to leave early to-night. They allow us an hour off every month, for shopping. Not that she means to shop, she says. But her Boy has got an hour off too. Her Boy has a car, and in the summer she's going to learn to drive it. He's in Everyman's, I believe, though I haven't tracked him down yet. And he's just got a rise, says Miss Lamb. So one hopes that he'll come up to the scratch soon, and marry her. Meanwhile, of course, she pays into the Superannuation Fund, because she'll get it out when she marries. It's as good a way of saving as any other. And either way, she's safe.

Miss Watts, the other typist, is older. She might be thirty-five or thirty or even twenty-eight. It depends on the time of day, and the weather, and the light in which she's standing, and whether anything pleasant is liable to happen, like the rain stopping at lunch-time. She doesn't seem to have a Boy, or if she has she's more reticent about him. Perhaps, at thirty-five (or thirty) financial security is the only thing that matters. But I doubt it. And I'm twenty-seven already.

Do you remember how you railed once against the mentality which demands and gets a safe job for forty years, and is rewarded by a marble clock, suitably inscribed, on retiring at the end of the forty-first? Could there, by the way, be a more ghoulish gift?

Anyway, good-night,

HILARY

MARTIN'S RESTAURANT

Saturday, 1.30
September 19th

Oh, Basil, there *are* compensations! It's worth sleep-walking from nine to six all the week just to wake up on Saturday with half a day and a night and another day after that unquestionably one's own. I came out of Everyman's and watched all the other people with hockey sticks and skates and suit-cases tearing for buses. But I strolled, feeling marvellous. Rather as if I'd kicked off a tightish pair of shoes.

It's just petty-cash pleasure of course. I can count all the things that go to make it. Hours of idleness ahead; nothing heavy to carry; nowhere to go in a hurry; dry pavements underfoot; all the back-street restaurants to choose from, and most of Friday's envelope still in my bag.

God, I'm so happy! Isn't it absurd? I suppose we're so bottled up during the week that Saturday's uncorking is apt to let off a colossal head of excitement. Set down on paper, though, I expect it all just looks rather tiresome. I wish I had you here. It's such a waste being happy alone. Happiness won't hoard, either. It isn't the least use trying to keep it for the next black mood. It won't even keep overnight.

Here's my lunch. A rump steak with crisped potatoes, and green things, because of your food lectures first: biscuits, Camembert cheese, black coffee and a cigarette coming.

. . . .

Those dots mean that I've eaten the rump steak (bi-manually). Cheese and biscuit stage now; so I can write again. Oh – *writing*! Shall I rush into the Post Office next door and put through a trunk call to Edinburgh? I suppose not. It would spoil Mrs MacQueen's Saturday afternoon so to know that your young woman had rung up from London (the wickedness of it!) when you were out. I don't know that talking's much good either on second thoughts. Perhaps there isn't any way of making contact. It's alarming, sometimes, to think of all the other things there are in your life besides me; and all so gravely important. But you know I adore you to be busy and talked about as the coming authority on pre-natal metabolism.

I love calling for you at the Medical School and watching your students crash out with their note-books full of your ideas. I'm blown out with pride when you come up to me and dust the chalk off your fingers on to the sleeve of my coat. Oh, Basil, fake up a conference quite soon and come up to London, and dine at length with all the European authorities on obstetrics and take me out to supper afterwards in some minor pub.

Well, in the meantime there's this week-end. I shall go down to the Embankment after I've posted this, and walk as far as Chelsea. Water and thin sunlight and spotted plane trees spilling leaves into it. Pleasant. There was frost last night. Then I'll buy bread and fruit and chocolate at one of the little shops which don't close on Saturday, and take a bus back to the Minerva after tea. I've got three books for the week-end, but this evening I shan't mind doing all the save-sixpence jobs: stocking washing (surreptitious, because of the notices about washing of garments. One wraps the Lux in a bath-towel, usually upside down and leaving an accusing, paper-chase trail).

After that, dull letters, even bills; shoe-cleaning; a book and a cigarette to make up for it all afterwards. Ten hours in bed ... breakfast just when I feel like it and where I wake up.

I'm going to eat rolls and fruit and chocolate instead of going downstairs. There's always Eno's if I'm taken with thirst. I won't move till eleven.

If it's sunny I'll go out for an hour to watch the dogs and ducks swimming in the Serpentine. If not, not. And after lunch I shall read …

I may write to you again, too.

Love, darling,

HILARY

PS – Now I know what people mean by 'A month of Sundays.' Heaven!

PART I – AUTUMN

MINERVA
Saturday Evening

September 19th

DEAREST FAMILY,

I've washed six pairs of stockings and darned three, ironed two blouses and two sets of collars and cuffs, and run yards of elastic into everything I could lay hands on. Laundry's such a fierce item that I'm going to try to do it myself. But I thought I'd begin gradually.

Thank you for the biscuits and cigarettes and most appropriate Lux and the money for a library subscription. Such intelligent presents, as if you'd both worked in London on £2:10:0 a week and knew just what it won't run to! I've eaten some biscuits and used the Lux and smoked two cigarettes, and taken out a subscription (Fiction C offered to the Staff at a reduced rate) from Everyman's Library.

Don't worry about the hours of work. They're long, but at present nobody could call the work I do intellectual or exacting. I mean, it oughtn't to kill anybody merely to copy hundreds of people's names and addresses from the library folders (where we keep the lists of books the subscribers want sent to them) on to the labels which go out with the books. And that's all I do so far. So I don't think you need be anxious. At least two-thirds of my brain is free to think about irrelevant things, such as new rooms and plans for the week-end. (Though if more than two-thirds of my attention wanders, very odd things happen to the labels.)

I don't think, incidentally, that I'm going to stay at the Minerva much longer. If you're working in London it's exasperating to come too much in contact with people who're merely living there. I don't see anybody at breakfast of course, but their talk at dinner is all about bridge parties and charity and the people they'd met in the Park. If I lived in rooms I needn't hear them.

I'm going to spend this weekend in utter laziness; but next Saturday I shall interview landladies. Can you give me any idea of the sort of questions one asks? What does a room look like when it is:

(*a*) Damp?

(*b*) Verminous?

(*c*) Unventilated?

After the profound interest I took in the Housing Problem during my second year at Oxford you'd think that some of the details would have stuck in the memory. But I'd be grateful for all the practical points with which you could stiffen my theoretical knowledge before next Saturday.

And now I think I'll go to bed. It's wonderfully soothing to know that I can stay there to-morrow morning for AS LONG AS I LIKE.

Much love,

HILARY

PART I - AUTUMN

THE MINERVA
Wednesday

September 23rd

BASIL RAINFORD, Esq:

DEAR SIR,

Herewith we beg to enclose the penultimate paragraph of our previous communication of Saturday's date. This page was inadvertently omitted; it had become detached and was not discovered (under the wash-stand by an interested chambermaid) until the letter of which it was part had been despatched. For this oversight we trust that you will accept our apologies, together with the assurance that everything in our power will be done to prevent the recurrence of such a mishap.

Have you ever noticed, Basil, how Commerce jibs at the simple statement? Circumlocution creeps into one's blood. Nothing is ever just 'lost' though it may – and often does 'become detached' and is in consequence 'temporarily mislaid.' We commence ... communicate ... insert ... query ... indicate ... proceed ...But on the other hand we even things up by talking about Jan ... and Feb ... and corres ... and sub ... and memo ... and advert ... and par ... Like a man in top hat and shirt sleeves, it takes getting used to. Sometimes we make 'slight slips'; 'some assistant' is a useful scapegoat for an 'inexplicable oversight', even for a 'gross blunder' (committed, more often than not, by the person composing the letter). It's a good game. Played occasionally. But think what it must do to your way of thinking after twenty years. Miss Sparling's an expert at it. Her mind must be incapable of unstereotyped thought. Except, perhaps, her dislike of me, which is a new and most luxuriant growth. But then, of course, she's one of those trap-mouthed women who'd rather wrangle than not.

Talking of Miss Sparling, I've disgraced myself to-day. Not irrevocably, Mr Simpson assures me. Still, quite prominently, as usual. Monday morning began it. The room was cold and the clock-hands seemed to have stuck somewhere between nine and ten. Label-writing became more than I could bear. It does, you know, very soon. At first it's a game; then it's just dull; but after two hours it's so gruesomely boring that it's not to be borne. I always wonder how Miss Hopper gets through the day at all, even though she does choose people's Books for the Brain. She seems to do nothing much but 'check' the things I've done already. She looks to see that the addresses are right and the labels in the proper books, and if the cardboard library folders have been written up properly and filed in the right drawers. She watches me, too, quite a lot. It's sometimes unnerving. The other day she said: 'I do like to watch you write, you know. You do it so easily. You must have done ever such a lot of it.'

But to-day I suddenly felt that I couldn't bear to scratch on in the usual way that meant reaching the bottom of the pile of books to be sent out somewhere in the middle of the afternoon. So I worked furiously and as fast as I dared. When I'd finished that pile I filed all the library folders I could find, tidied everything I could see, filled Miss Hopper's ink-pot and unobtrusively went to lunch.

I only got as far as the cloakroom. I was pulling on my hat in front of that mirror when I heard Miss Hopper behind me. She said: 'Aren't you feeling quite well?' I said: 'Oh, yes, thank you.' And smiled quite kindly at her because I'd done such a lot of work and was feeling proud. Then I picked up my bag and tried to get past.

'You're never leaving the *building*?' said Miss Hopper. 'You can't, you know, not without Sister or Miss Ward give you leave.'

PART I – AUTUMN

'But how does anybody ever get out?' I said as I pulled on my gloves. 'One must lunch, after all. I've never asked Sister yet.'

'But you can't lunch at half-past eleven when your time is one,' said Miss Hopper.

'But it *is* one o'clock,' I said. (Though I had a horrid, sudden doubt.)

Miss Hopper just said: 'Come downstairs and look at the clock.'

She showed me three, and they all bore her out. It was all very public and shaming. For once the typists stopped: Mr Simpson came up and murmured: Miss Dowland said: 'If you bring chocolate, dear, it helps.'

They all hustled me back to my labels, and for the next hour and a half I just obstinately *sat*, though I may have written two more. At five minutes to one Mr Simpson came up and said that he'd see I wasn't idle. So after lunch he gave me a list of books that I could type for him. It was nice to get to know their names, wasn't it?

I spent the afternoon over his list. It wasn't altogether wilful meandering, either. I just couldn't get the prices to add up right, and whenever I was half-way up the shillings column Miss Hopper sent me to get something for her or a packer brought me back one of my more illegible labels and I had to begin at the bottom again.

I have to remind myself quite often these days that I'm doing a job and justifying my existence, and helping patriots to Buy British; and oftener still that in the natural course of events it won't last for ever or even for very many months. Because I'd hate to be Miss Lamb and type hundreds of form letters a day; letters to say how obliged we are for an esteemed order, and how we beg to hand people an invoice therewith, and that we can't imagine what's happened to their goods, but we will take the matter up with the Postal Authorities.

If anyone wants to do this sort of work really well or happily she has to be either so stupid that elementary detail is enough for her or else so efficient that she hardly needs to think of it at all. I'm neither. So, at the moment, Basil, dear, it hardly looks as if I'd make my mark. There's nothing remarkable about this sort of work unless you do it badly.

And yet, it *is* work, and masses of people haven't got it and would probably jump at it. Oughtn't that dog-in-possession feeling to be enough to satisfy a girl?

What a Mondayish letter! I'd better go and have a bath. That's to say, supposing I can afford another sixpence. And *that* reminds me, I'm going to look for a room somewhere else. Not, of course, altogether because I grudge the sixpences. But when one uses hot baths as pick-me-ups in the evenings and for practical purposes in the mornings as well, it begins to come expensive. Besides, I like the hotel even less on second thoughts: I don't like the people who are unfriendly in an Anglo-Indian way, and the people who insist on being friendly are worse. Besides, typists don't live in hotels: as far as I can make out they live with aged parents or in hostels, where you get a cubicle and bed-rock board for twenty-something shillings a week. I doubt if I could bear that, but if I'm to rent a small flat when my salary makes it possible, I've *got* to live on my week's earnings now. Twenty pounds sounds well, but it doesn't go far when one's furnishing – even two rooms and a cubby hole.

So I'm collecting information about all the people who let lodgings and can be recommended as respectable (remembering the Corset gentleman and his proposals) for a working girl of just the most moderate means. There should be lots of names on the list by the end of this week: on Saturday I'll go and look them up.

Tell me, what about the book? Oughtn't it to be emerging into the proof stage quite soon? Of course I shall want to see it, just as soon as there is anything to see, even those galley things like fly-papers which are so difficult to read and so exhausting for the arms unless one could become a fly for the occasion and have them hung up to crawl over. You know, dear, that any opinion I may form will be entirely valueless, but I shall understand (remembering) the bits you explained to me in the summer. And I shall enjoy strewing those galleys about my room and nonchalantly inviting people in to see me.

Oh, darling, I must tell you, Mr Simpson intercepted me when I was creeping home at six o'clock and said that I was please not to worry about my slight slip this morning. He did hope that I wouldn't let it get on my mind. Bless him!

      And you,

      HILARY

MINERVA

Saturday, September 26th

OH, MY DEAR,

Hunting rooms is almost as bad as hunting jobs. And quite the world's worst way of spending any Saturday. I set out with my list, very cross, and went grandly to look at Ladies Clubs. But of course they were much too expensive. And, anyway, I dislike their elderly boarding-school atmosphere. So I went in to the place which advertised Bed-sitting-rooms for Ladies instead. All dingy and unreasonably far from bus stops. I tramped about with my list, grudging the September sunshine that would have been lovely on nearly everything, but which showed up holes in carpets and dirt on windows and lines on landladies' faces. Dust danced in it and smells rose through it and I turned tail in the middle. I dashed down to the Embankment to smoke a cigarette and watch seagulls. When I felt better I stroked off the names of the places I'd been to and started off again.

And now I've found some sort of a hole for myself. It belongs to a house that provides homes for Ladies Only – all sorts of impoverished ladies from midwives to ministers' widows. It's run by the inevitable Colonel's wife who's come down in the world.

Something obscure seems to have happened to that Colonel: she doesn't like him mentioned except for purposes of advertisement. No palm-pots here, of course: you walk into a narrow passage that smells of damp oilcloth and mice. But not, thank heaven, of meals either past, present or to come.

At the end of the passage there's a door marked OFFICE in amateurish printing. Behind this the Colonel's wife lives, in a bed-sitter like everybody else; only, because her room is also the place of business there's more sit and less bed about it than most. Of course, the japanned screen shouts wash-stand at anyone, but the divan and the arm-chair and the bureau with its elephant-foot letter-weights and its blotting-pad are most convincing. The Colonel's wife was inclined to be rather Anglo-Indian with me at first, especially as most of the rooms cost more than I'd decided to afford. But just as I had given up hope she owned to one at seventeen shillings a week.

'It mayn't be quite as comfy as the others,' she said. 'But then – well, we can't have *everything* for nothing in this world, can we?'

All the same, I like it. It's small and down the basement stairs, but there's an antique kitchen stove which nobody has taken the trouble to screen, and I shall be able to stow away any amount of things in its ovens. I like the white walls, the red cotton curtains, and the shabby red carpet. And I like the narrow panes of glass above the ex-area door and the foreshortened view of passing ankles. I prefer my bed to *be* a bed, which is fortunate. For seventeen shillings a week one doesn't get a divan. That sort of elegance costs twenty-five and sixpence. There's a basket-chair which creaks and reminds me of Lady Hilda's. And a table with one leg shorter than the rest. But mercifully the bath (which is miles away on the first floor), the gas-fire and electric light are penny-in-the-slot. I'm all for the copper standard and I'm moving in tomorrow. Address, 23 Burford Street, WC.

Basil, won't it be fun when you can get a week-end off? I shall make you take me out and provide an expensive dinner followed by Turkish coffee and old brandy. Then we'll dance, and afterwards I'll bring you back to my basement and give you herring-roes personally cooked over a pennyworth of gas. When will you come? Soon, please.

HILARY

PART I - AUTUMN

23 BURFORD STREET

October 2nd

MY DEAR,

A good day; we were paid, and your letter was waiting for me when I got home. Such a nice, partisan letter too. You said all the things that I secretly wanted to hear about the absurdity of an educated woman working at menial jobs for a mere pittance and living in a basement on a few shillings a week, about the waste of making people like me write labels that a Board School child would probably do better, anyway. (This not so welcome, perhaps. But true.) Your indignation was most infectious. I was quite furious myself as I read your views on vitiated atmospheres and impossible hours, and things being different for me because I wasn't used to them.

But on the other hand, Basil, it's just *because* I'm not used to them that things like living in a basement, earning two pounds ten a week and budgeting every penny, are amusing. (On Pay Day.) I suppose it's not a fair test of this sort of life, either. I can always run away. They – the other people with basements and nine-to-six and two pounds ten a week – can't. You remember the story that Byron shut himself up in one of those dungeons for a while to get the atmosphere for *The Prisoner of Chillon?* I always thought that was cheating: all he had to do was to yell and he'd have been set free.

So you needn't worry quite so indignantly about me. I *could* run away. But I don't want to. Which, as you'll tell me if I don't mention it first, is just sheer, thrawn, wicked pride. No, it isn't, either. Not entirely. I do want to go on supporting myself, unaided, during this bad year. Then I needn't panic at the thought of letting you support me for the rest of my life.

Well, we were paid to-day, and I felt better afterwards. This time I brazenly counted the money in my envelope twice, instead of shoving it into my bag as if I couldn't take time from my labours to make sure of the hire. Then on the way home I called in at one of those sub-restaurants where they feed people; (just food: no frills). I had an enormous bowl of soup; a cut from the joint with two vegs; an apple dumpling; bread and cheese and coffee. Then, over a cigarette, I worked out the week's budget.

I've never kept accounts before, except at school and under compulsion. But I'm proud of my budget. Everything is accounted for: nothing remains. Here it is:

£	s.	d.	
	17	0	This room.
	3	6	Breakfasts at sixpence each. Quite good. (Even sardines.)
	9	6	Lunches. I find I simply can't do without one-and-sixpence worth of lunch when I'm working. But I can manage on a shilling at the week-end.
1		3	Tea. Daily, at threepence, not counting week-ends, when it's drawn from personal stores.
	7	0	Dinners.
	2	0	Household. Tooth-paste, soap, Lux, face-cream, powder. (They mount up most damnably. I buy Lux one week, tooth-paste the next and so on. But my family has a heavenly way of unexpectedly replenishing household stores which I gratefully encourage.)
	3	0	Emergency Fund. That covers things like having shoes soled. It also goes towards

			new stockings on the weeks when there haven't been any other emergencies. Once the entire fund went on a taxi when I was late and reckless. But I got about a pound's worth of peace of mind for those three shillings, while I sat back and watched other people fighting on to the buses.
1	8		Buses. I'm definitely against walking now, what with shoe leather and scarcity of time.
1	4		Fruit. Your orders.
2	6		Gas fire. Baths. Electric light.
1	3		Insurance (Health and so on). Sorely grudged.
2	10	0	QED

I did that sum this evening over the wreckage of my big meal. Then I took half a crown out of the Emergency Fund to pay for it (it's to be hoped that nothing dire happens this week, as it now contains sixpence), and came home, feeling good.

But, for all that, the budget isn't a really reliable joke. I don't suppose, for instance, that it'll stand much repetition. And I've been rather dreary until to-day – not getting as much fun as usual out of living on £2:10:0 a week. Of course I can comfort myself by writing to you about it, but sometimes I almost forget that it isn't really a trap that I've got to run round for the rest of my life. When I say that I look on you as a bolt-hole it isn't as rude as it sounds.

I know I shan't spend my life this way. I *won't*. But the others, Miss Hopper and Miss Watts and Mildred Lamb, will. And they know it. It's the only way they can be safe; sure of a place to sleep in, food, and those tidy, monotonous clothes. But they pay *so* much more for that safety (in things that aren't money), than the basic two pounds ten a week.

The worst of earning one's living, Basil, is that it leaves so little time over to live in. During the winter you've got to hand over the eight daylight hours to *Everyman's*, and only keep the twilight bits at each end. And most of them go to waste in sleep.

In fact, I've been drowning myself in *lacrimae rerum* all week. And it rained too: I hated my stove because nobody cooked meals on it any more: I hated the red carpet because the floor underneath was stone and damp: I minded the rain coming in under the ex-area door because it made a pool, and my one good pair of shoes was standing in it next morning. I couldn't get to sleep most nights because the sheets were horrid. The darns scratched me. One blanket was too short and the other too narrow and both were dirty. I couldn't tuck my coat round me because it was damp. Last night my only two pennies flickered out simultaneously in the gas fire and the electric light at five minutes past eight, and I spilt my supper half-pint of milk as I was getting into bed.

This morning Mrs Hemming, who's the 'service' included in my rent, mourned over the mess.

'Does seem a shyme, don't it miss? 'Owever I'll get this grate clean I do *not* know, and me with twenty in the 'ouse to do for. Not that it's the work I object to, miss. It's the waste. It may be nothing to you, miss, if you'll excuse my saying so. No doubt you can go and get a good meal when you like. But if you was goin' to throw it away, you might 'ave given it to them as needed it first. Not that I'm thinking of meself. But there's them girls upstairs. You get a bed to yourself when all's said and done, but if you lay three in a bed and often 'aven't enough milk to make a cup of tea with, let alone kippers and such' – at this point she picked up the remains of mine by the tail and threw it into the dust-bin as if I'd stolen it – 'for your supper – well, you look twice before you throw away a 'ole 'alfpint, that makes work for others in the clearin' of it up. No offence, of course, but there's no good saying one thing and thinking another, as Mr Hemming always says.'

Still, she *has* cleared it up. And I've put threepence in the gas all at once, left the fire on while I spent twopence on a bath, piled all my coats on the bed and sagged into it, warm and well fed, with your letter. You could have chosen, my lamb, between a snippet of a reply posted this evening which would greet you with your breakfast to-morrow, and a long letter which won't arrive before the last post. I thought I'd choose for you (it's raining), and I hope you'll approve. To-night I'm a luxurious animal: I refuse to get my feet wet again. I'm just gloating over the comfort of being warm and loved.

You do love me, Basil, don't you? Oh, I know; but I'd just like to see it in writing again. You were so voluble over my wrongs that you forgot to mention it.

Bless you, anyway,

HILARY

23 BURFORD STREET

October 8th

BASIL, MY LAMB,

Something actually happened to-day. Something startling, I mean, not like the things which keep on happening all the time without anyone being the better for them. It was during the lunch hour: Miss Hopper had gone early – she has a queasy stomach, she says, and can't do with a Long Morning. So she goes to lunch at twelve-fifteen. Very useful. Anyway, there I was, alone at her table, and, by the mercy of heaven, working hard. In other words, carefully 'inserting' a card into the index every five minutes. (At that rate I can make the job last for an hour.)

Suddenly there was a pause in the typing; then it went on again like gun fire. The whole atmosphere crackled. Obviously some sort of an Olympian had come in.

I didn't actually look up, but I felt him come down the narrow gangway between book-cases and tables, and all the books that were half on and half off the tables fell off them at once. I thought, 'Well, *I*'m safe, anyway. He can't know I exist.' So I put three cards into the index at once and kept up that sort of terrorised efficiency till I thought he must be well away. Then I looked up, and he'd stopped six inches off, staring at me. *Very* god like. (But clean-shaven.)

He said: 'Miss Hopper, can you explain this?' And he floated a letter down on to my index cards. (They were wet, of course, but I daren't protest. An efficient woman would have had blotting paper.)

I grabbed the letter, and said: 'Certainly.'

He looked again. 'Are you Miss Hopper?'

PART I - AUTUMN

I said: 'Certainly not!'

He said: 'Then you can't. Most annoying.' (Very short.) I said: 'Why not?' And kept hold of the letter, though he seemed inclined to grab it back. It was the sort I've met quite a lot lately, tilted, bad-tempered handwriting that crawled up one page in the third person and down the opposite side in the first. In the middle there were exclamation marks, and the writer demanded her money back.

I didn't actually understand what it was all about, but mercifully the name and address came first, and were followed by something about unsuitable literature and crass carelessness. Then I remembered the 'biographies with your butcher meat' phrase, and guessed that some Rational Reader must have been given kippers and Marie Corelli when they'd ordered Galsworthy and caviare. I stopped being frightened then and consulted the card-index in a dazed but competent way, found Mrs Pillington-Smythe's card, picked it out without the usual shower of adherent, next-door tickets, and read out all the particulars on it.

The Minor Prophet just looked at me, and said, 'Well?' and, 'How *do* you explain it?' So I read the letter through again and took it in this time.

'Mrs Pillington-Smythe' (it said) 'is amazed that any firm of your standing should encourage the sale of books which can only undermine the morals of the country. If certain people choose to demand such literature (save the mark) that is their own affair. But surely, even in these degenerate days, youth is still sacred. As the Headmistress of a school to which many prominent people send their daughters you will appreciate that I am in a position of some trust.

'I subscribed to your Service on the understanding that you would keep my school supplied with what is best in modern literature. I particularly explained that if fiction be sent at all, it must be only such fiction as leaves the reader the better for having read it, such fiction as she may confidently put into the hands of the daughters of prominent people who attend her school. Mrs Pillington-Smythe gave a list of her preferences, which included Biography, Travel, Memoirs and History, in that order. She understood that she would be supplied with select literature only, and considers that her confidence has been abused. She would be obliged if Messrs. Everyman would refund the amount which she paid them in advance.'

I said: 'Yes, that must be *For One Night Only*. I did ask Miss Hopper if it was quite safe for Mrs Pillington-Smythe and her girl's school, but she said that they always had the Book of the Week, and if a book was the Book of the Week, it was always Quite Nice.'

'Yes, yes, but what do you propose to do now?' said the Minor Prophet. I was tempted to say that I'd leave it to Miss Hopper, but with that eye upon me, some sort of action seemed imperative.

'She ought to have a very careful letter,' I suggested. 'We might say that these books are kept solely for a small clientele with advanced – I mean peculiar – views. And while we may deplore their tastes …' (The Minor Prophet finished the sentence as I'd hoped.) 'We are nevertheless obliged to satisfy their requirements.' His voice wobbled a little, but when I looked hopefully up at him his face was grimmer than ever. 'And then,' I said, 'we'd send a much more expensive and extra pure book in exchange – no further charge, of course.'

He said: 'Possibly. Write the letter.' As an afterthought, he asked: Did I type? Good. No shorthand? Serious disadvantage. Well, I'd better type out the letter and send it up for his signature. That was all he'd come to say. I could tell Miss Hopper that I was acting on his instructions. Then he walked out. But of course I hadn't the remotest idea who he was, so I went up to Miss Dowland and asked her. She said: 'Oh, I *thought* you didn't know. That was Mr Grant.' (The man who made up those rhymes. I wrote about them. No wonder he was furious about a brain and bread-basket blunder.)

I said: 'Oh, was it. Thank you,' and wondered what she had on her mind. She went on talking and seemed to have got lost in a sentence about business etiquette, and it all being so strange at first. Eventually, she got round to it, and it appeared that I ought to have called him 'Sir' and she did hope that I wouldn't mind her pointing it out: she couldn't help hearing that I'd never said it: I'd got such a clear voice: it wasn't as if she'd listened. I was please not to think anything of the kind and not to worry, anyway, because he'd know I was new to the business and never dream of holding it up against me.

Well, that hadn't occurred to me as a possibility, and I didn't let it prey on my mind. I made up a really lovely letter to Mrs Pillington-Smythe, full of apology and flattery and an appeal to her superior insight (not too good English, because that would have annoyed her but with all the best commercial circumlocutions). I wound up with a long sentence of abnegation in which I said that we perfectly understood that, in the circumstances, she would like to have her money back. We were putting the matter through at once, and in the meantime we trusted that she would accept a copy of *The Roof Tree of the World* at thirty shillings, without, of course, any further charge. It's been remaindered at five, but who's to know? Not Mrs P-S. I enjoyed writing that letter. I wasn't quite sure of the placatory technique, so I asked Miss Dowland about credit notes and special deliveries and she told me. But the typing! I did it five times, incredibly slowly, and each time I made a mistake nearer the end.

Miss Dowland came up when I was finishing the fifth copy and asked me whether I'd like her to type it for me, as it was so difficult, wasn't it, once one let a thing like that get on one's nerves. And of course Mr Grant was ever so particular. I said, 'Thank you. I'll manage.' And put an irrelevant question mark into my still unblemished fifth version. Miss Dowland said: 'And he's got a wicked eye for erasures.' Mercifully, after that she went away, and I champed through the blistering letter once again, took five minutes over the envelope, wrote a little note of explanation and put the thing in the messenger girl's box for Mr Grant.

And that, I hope, will be the last of that. But at least I've never known an afternoon at Everyman's go so quickly as this one; nor have I ever worked so hard. When I'd finished and came back to Miss Hopper and her labels, she said: 'You've just time for half an hour's work. All that time off! Gets me so behind, you know.' Time off! Time off! I ask you!

I went home muttering, and pushed my way on to a bus in front of two innocent people who had their arms too full of parcels to push back. 'These shop girls,' said one of them, and the other said, 'Tck-tck, no manners!' as the bus left them on the pavement.

There was a letter from the family waiting for me. They said, among other things, that you'd been round, interviewing Father about something encyclopædic, and afterwards stayed to dinner. They'd liked that. I wonder if you'd still have been escorted to the door afterwards by Father in the old way if I'd been there, or whether my official standing gives me the right to drag a usurping parent back by the coat tails. Probably.

They said you had a cold again. I'm sorry. Does that Mr. MacQueen look after you in the competent Scots way with whisky toddy and mustard baths and stockings round the throat and hot bottles and blackcurrant tea? There's no fun in a cold unless people treat it like pneumonia.

Please report progress.

Love,

HILARY

Covering Note

To Mr Grant

Memo

Herewith the letter of apology to Mrs Pillington-Smythe. I understand that in an emergency it is permissible to employ a special messenger to deliver goods. I have done this, and hope you consider the action justified.

I know that there need be no delay, strictly speaking, in putting through a credit note. But I thought that it might give Mrs PillingtonSmythe time to do something gracious – even to change her mind about cancelling her library subscription.

Pending this I have marked her folder as follows:

CAUTION – SCHOOL

EXCLUSIVE: NON-FICTION

(No Sex)

From:

HILARY FANE

Book Floor

October 8th, 1931

EVERYMAN'S STORES

For use in inter-departmental correspondence only

From M G Grant *To* Staff Supervisor
October 9th, 1931

Subject Junior Clerk, 537 (H Fane), Book Floor, Clerical

Memo

Her record (education and previous posts) seems to indicate that she is fitted for a better position than that of Junior Clerk.

This is confirmed by an incident of yesterday's date. A most serious complaint in connection with our new Rational Reading Service was brought to my notice. In Miss Hopper's absence, Miss Fane was able to give a lucid explanation of the occurrence. She also showed herself capable of handling the situation and drafted a suitable letter (2 erasures) for my signature.

I doubt her proficiency as a clerk (she has no shorthand), but consider that she might with advantage be given more responsible work.

I should welcome your views.

MGG

SN/MGG

BUSINESS AS USUAL

EVERYMAN'S STORES

For use in inter-departmental correspondence only

From Staff Supervisor *To* Mr Grant

October 9th, 1931

Subject Junior Clerk, 537 (H Fane), Book Floor, Clerical

Memo

Miss Fane is a very good type. Had she training and experience she might be well fitted for promotion, but she is handicapped by lack of both.

She was engaged, on a month's trial, at short notice to replace Clerk 536, Miss Pim (absent appendicitis). I have had no complaints about her work, though I hear from Sister Smith that she is not well adapted to routine and does not make use of the canteen or other social amenities.

I regret that you should not find her typing good. Unless she is thoroughly proficient, she can hardly be given promotion.

Shall I speak to her and suggest a night school?

MEW

BT/MEW

PART I – AUTUMN

EVERYMAN'S STORES

For use in inter-departmental correspondence only

From M G Grant

To Staff Supervisor
October 9th, 1931

Subject Junior Clerk, 537 (H Fane), Book Floor, Clerical

Memo

Certainly not. We have too many shorthand typists and not enough intelligent assistants.

When Miss Pim returns to her duties, arrange for Miss Fane to have a few weeks on the Selling Staff in the Book Department. She might then go on to the Library.

Please obtain reports on her work from time to time and pass them to me.

MGG

SN/MGG

23 BURFORD STREET

October 11th

DEAREST FAMILY,

What's all this about my being Alone in London? What have you been reading? And what made you think of those possible friends for me who might be lurking, unfriended, in Everyman's? I'm not in the least solitary, you know, except on purpose.

But I *like* being alone now and then. Not morbidly, just quite simply, like Kipling's cat. It's a useful, inexpensive taste. It'd be so inconvenient to be like one of the few young people in the Minerva who spent every Friday evening in terror that she'd be left alone for an hour over the week-end. The whole lounge used to echo with her miserable telephoning.

No, I haven't been to see Aunt Bertha. And I'm most certainly not going just at present. She doesn't know I'm in London. And I'd be obliged if you'd not tell her. I haven't the sort of hat that'd keep me in countenance in Cadogan Square. And even if I had the hat, no coat and gloves and shoes, and handbag and umbrella would coincide enough for a poor relation to visit a very rich one without discomfort.

There are lots of ex-Oxford people in London, you know, and I see them occasionally, more often by accident than by telephone. And, anyway, I know they're there if I feel social. So you needn't worry.

About my room. I think it's a successful change. There's so much more fun in being on one's own than herded, and as a place it's amusing. Warm, you know, because it's not very big, and odd because it's below the street level, though it's not a basement, of course, because I have a perfectly good window that opens. It's wire-netted to prevent cats from coming in, and that's a blessing. Much as I adore cats, I don't find myself drawn to the average London slum-stinker. (Not that Burford Street's a slum. Far from it: it's a most respectable, clerkly neighbourhood.)

Basil says that he spent a very interesting evening at University Close this week. Do I recognise the festival described in Thursday's letter, when Daddy and Basil held a two-hour discussion on pre-Hellenic civilisations and you thought out three ways of arranging the drawing-room furniture when the spring-cleaning came round?

The water for my hot-bottle is boiling, so I'll stop. Notice how I surround myself with all the comforts of home.

Very much love to you both,

HILARY

23 BURFORD STREET

October 12th
Really Early
(Before getting up.)

DARLING,

How sweet of you to write at once. Yes, it would be grand if I'd really impressed the Minor Prophet favourably, wouldn't it? But so far he's vouchsafed no sign.

I was slightly cowed by your lecture on efficiency. But, you know, I am efficient in important things: it's only that I do so grudge spending energy on mechanical work. I have to spend so much more of it than other people, and I do the work so much worse in the end. It's galling, to say the least of it, to do badly what an elementary school child half my age would do really well. So I try. I try incredibly hard, to be quite honest. I see that labels have to be well written – by somebody. Only I doubt if that person is – or can be – me. I'm getting quite good, though, at NEAT PRINTING.

It's when the future seems to present an unending vista of neatly printed labels that I quail. However …

It's an enormous relief to know that your cold's better. I was horror-struck yesterday by the thought that it might be turning into flu: I remembered Mistress MacQueen and the two husbands she had buried. So easy just to let you slip away with pneumonia.

It's a mercy that Arnold Grieves is back; much less dreary and laborious for you. And I'm glad that he likes your book so much. But I don't think you ought to give up golf at the week-end even for the blessedly important final proofs of *The Prime Factors in Pre-Natal Metabolism*. You don't get enough fresh air as it is. (Though heaven knows that nobody's practice is further from his precept than a really eminent surgeon's.) What you really want, of course, is a secretary – but I don't suggest myself for the job. You need Mechanical Efficiency in the highest degree. Why not find someone who will type very fast and set out your figures regimentally for you? You've no idea what a comfort it would be. Wait till I come to Edinburgh. I'll find you an unprepossessing pearl.

The main point is that I implore you not to overwork. And – but it's after eight o'clock, and I ought not only to be up and eating my breakfast, but actually on my way to the bus stop.

I'll finish this later, when I've written another thousand labels.

Bless you.

(I shall be quite IMPOSSIBLY LATE …)

Later – I was. And my name went down in a book which Mr Simpson bore away with him, I believe to check with the clocking machine's damning record. I fancy there's a penalty, but so far Nemesis has not shown herself.

BUSINESS AS USUAL

EVERYMAN'S STORES

For use in inter-departmental correspondence only

From Staff Supervisor *To* Clerk 537, H Fane
Book Floor

October 12th, 1931

Subject Transfer to Selling Staff

Memo

Miss Pim, whom you are replacing, will be returning to her duties on Wednesday, October 14th.

You will then be required to serve in the Book Department.

Kindly see Sister Smith about your transfer to Selling Staff and arrange for a staff dress (Blue, model B.501 Junior Saleswoman) to be put through on a rush order.

Also note that your number will be changed from C.537 to S.(T)801.

MEW

BT/MEW

Hilary to Basil (Contd.)

23 BURFORD STREET

My dear, things have happened. Oh, nothing spectacular. And quite unconnected with the Minor Prophet's visitation, I'm afraid. Merely what they call a 'Meemo' (with the 'e' long as in the pronoun). It comes from the Staff Supervisor: it says I must go and sell books next week, and therefore must have a new dress and a new number. All quite willy-nilly, of course.

I don't object, particularly. After all, I can't go lower (unless they make me a cleaner and tell me to scrub floors). So let's suppose I'm going higher. There doesn't seem to be any reason for the upheaval, though, except that the Appendicitis Case is coming back after six weeks exactly, as you said. Anyway, they haven't sacked me in consequence. Which is something.

And I escaped from my labels for an hour this morning. Half of the time went in waiting to see Sister, who says that she 'hasn't the ghost of a notion why they're changing me and wouldn't tell me if she had. The idea!' And she did wish I'd try to be a bit more sociable. She wouldn't forbid me lunching out, if I *must* do it, but why didn't I use the Canteen more? I'd get a real good diet there and the other girls would help to take my attention off myself. She knew what it was: I felt a bit out of things. But I must be careful not to give myself airs, though I might come from a better home than most. And I ought to have an arch support put in my left shoe, otherwise my foot would be flat in a week. And before I went into the Shop would I please to kindly have my hair trimmed and my stockings drawn tight with the seam straight. I gather that a hole in either heel is a capital offence. Heaven help me, Basil. I shan't survive a week.

Sister Smith inspects the Selling Staff from time to time; I suppose to gauge the depth of rouge on the cheeks and the flatness of the feet. All my points went down again to-day on another card, and the date on which I'm to get my new dress went with them. They take two days to make it. Rush Order. And in six months, Sister says, I'll be due for another. 'It may go for another three if you're careful.' I doubt it. If I don't spill my tea over it, someone else will.

But Sister Smith said it was my duty to the firm to get the last inch of wear out of that dress. Then, before I could be expected to agree, someone was dragged up to her door in a faint. She said: 'Dear, dear. That's the third this morning. This heat is *not* seasonable. Will you kindly move so that I can get at the Medicine Cupboard.' So I went.

I spent most of my lunch hour over that dress. (Staff Discount is only to be had between nine and ten or one and two.) I walked into the Inexpensive Gown Department on my way out (in my hat and coat) and said that I wanted something very special, because I didn't know how to begin about the Staff Dress. They fetched a Sales Manager to me, quite in a flutter. (Marvellous to be called 'Moddom' again, Basil!) But it didn't last. When she found out what I wanted she wasn't at all pleased. Apparently it damages the dignity to entertain employees unawares. She gave me just one look and called the youngest child in the department, indicating me with a little finger. And sailed away.

'Bitch!' said the child when she was approximately out of earshot. 'That Miss Methuen'd slit your throat as soon's look at you when her corns hurt her. Don't you mind. Bust … 34. The things she does you'd not believe. Lift your arms, dear. Waist … 26. Here, you're not breathing.' Then we started to giggle, and the Sales Manager loomed up round one of the show-cases. The child went on muttering things which may have been measurements into her Sales Book.

PART I – AUTUMN

'BITCH!' SAID THE CHILD.'

My dress was put down as S. (T) 801. Model B. (Rush Order.) Royal Blue. Junior Assistant. I chose the pattern out of the three possible ones. All hideous – jail-plain. Decorative effects are reserved for Senior Saleswomen and you can't command black satin and ruffles on the tail till you're a Sales Manager at least. I've to go for a fitting to-morrow. (In the lunch hour.)

The child said I'd be bound to find the life hard on the feet. 'It's something cruel, the first week or two. You try Radol. Sit with your feet in boiling water for ten minutes and it helps a lot.' (Kill or cure, presumably.) 'You'll have a bit of bother with your bills, I should think too.'

I shall. Sales Books have five carbons which must all be shot in different directions, customer, cashier, departmental records ... goodness knows where else. The customer is the only obvious person, and she's apt to crunch it up and leave it underfoot for you to pick up. (I've done it so often, in my customer days. But never again.) Then the child stopped in mid-sentence and said she mustn't waste any more of my time. Actually, she'd seen a customer, and fairly raced across the room to get ahead of the other visible assistant, who was a slow starter. Commission mounts up so.

So I've only got two more days of label-writing, Basil. Can you believe it? And I may be a very good saleswoman and Rise Rapidly. Anything may happen, after all. Turn again, Whittington!

Yours, on the ladder,

HILARY

PS – What about buying your medical books from Everyman's? The postage would be a mere trifle. And what is postage compared with our willing, expert service?

PPS – Mrs Pillington-Smythe has renewed her subscription. There!

PART I – AUTUMN

23 BURFORD STREET

October 14th

DARLING,

The first day's over. I'm derelict. My feet are seething in that bowl of Radol and my head is bloody but unbowed.

I started off, in my new Staff Dress and reached the Book Department, locally known as 'the shop', radiating brightness and efficiency (according to my lights).

It was disappointing to find that a day in the shop begins with a duster, just like a day of being Hopper's girl. And Mr Salt is there to see that you use it. He seemed disposed to be kind to me, though. Which is lucky, as he's quite an important person, nearly as important as fat Mr Hibbert who is really in charge of the department but spends most of his time sitting in a corner pencilling catalogues. Mr Hibbert's rather reticent at present, having just had his front teeth out. I always wondered what people did during the interregnum between sets. Mr Hibbert just carries on in a Trappist sort of way.

So it was Mr Salt who did the honours. It seems that it's one of his jobs to wield the pencil when underlings call out 'Sign, please'. He demonstrated the technique for my benefit behind the Children's Fiction. There's more in it than you'd think. One mustn't shout. But one must be heard. 'Clear, not raucous, Miss Fane. All a question of voice-production.' He was really very kind, but rather like the White Knight. You know, lots of patents; ways of fitting carbons into Sales Books at speed, working out those nightmarish sales summaries, and finding out the price of second-hand books by the hieroglyphics inside the cover. (T/R means 8/6, Basil. The Key Word's **PALMERSTON** in our shop.)

Then he walked me up and down pointing out landmarks: the Cash Desk, the Pocket Editions, the Latest Fiction, the Select Books of Travel, and the two discreet shelves for the classics and Marie Stopes. Somebody came up to say that one of his sales girls was ill (had gone to bed with a doctor's certificate was the term used). But at that point a customer came in: Mr Salt intercepted her: Mr Hibbert took off his bowler. The day had begun.

And how!

I sold books: lots of books. It's easy enough just to *sell* them: it only means being attentive and sympathetic and admiring and good-tempered and patient and unobtrusively determined. It's when you have to add in a hurry: there's the rub!

PART I – AUTUMN

Your pencil strays at unfortunate moments: and when you've taken ten minutes to tie up a parcel with a fretful customer almost snatching at the string the thing deliberately uncoils itself before he gets it to the lift.

The efficiency goes first. Then the brightness. Your shoes come undone: hairpins drop out – just like that. Everywhere. The new staff dress begins to droop. You make an effort for a lady with a train to catch and collide with an Olympian.

BUSINESS AS USUAL

After that, nothing matters. You are stricken with deafness and palsy at the sound of an order.

And when it is all over you crawl home and Cut off your Boots.

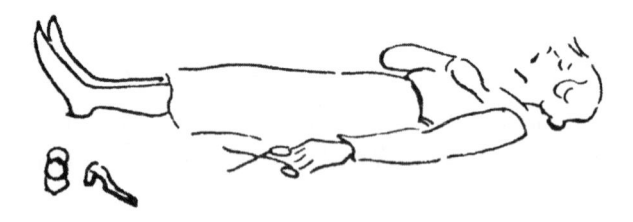

Will Radol work miracles? Or shall I go to work in bedroom slippers to-morrow?

Anyway, I 'took sixteen pounds' and Mr Salt's surprise was very comforting.

I love you, dear. But, oh, my FEET!

HILARY

PART I - AUTUMN

23 BURFORD STREET

October 17th

DEAREST FAMILY,

You remember that I came to Everyman's instead of someone who was ill? Well, the creature's had appendicitis rather quickly: she came back to work this week. Apparently I've managed to satisfy the management, because I'm not being flung out. The first I knew about it was a note transferring me to the Book Department of the Shop. It's a merciful change from writing people's addresses on labels, and I think I'm going to like it on the whole.

I've been there since Wednesday, and still feel a little uncertain about the addition of the longer bills. But I can find dictionaries and classics and detective stories and military biographies from their shelves without running to ask Mr Salt.

He, by the way, is one of the black-coated young men in office there, and he's given me most of my information. He said on my first morning that I would find the customers very agreeable. People who bought books were so much pleasanter than the ones who bought boots. I should have thought that even they had their off moments for soling and heeling, but I hadn't the heart to wreck his epigram. His spiritual home is Cambridge, but he's making a career of Commerce. And I think he quite likes his little distractions by the way. He's been most helpful, and perfectly right about the customers, so far. They've been very nice to me. I'm developing quite a fairy-godmotherish manner towards people looking for birthday presents. I beam on them and lead the way to the gift and special bindings (leather, tooled, from half a guinea upwards). On the other hand, I'm extremely understanding and helpful to the people who begin with, 'I want you to understand that in these times ...' Better a second-hand sale than none. There's rather a fascination, of course, in making somebody buy a guinea book when they'd meant to have one at half a crown.

Something rather amusing happened yesterday. I wasn't serving anybody, so when an odd customer strayed in I went to him. He'd a yellowish face and an eye-glass and a stick and an Inverness cape and a bull terrier, on a lead as prescribed.

I thought he was rather comic and old at first, but he had a lot of black hair and a quite undecrepit voice. Hopelessly puzzling. But he asked me for 'that book on Pre-Hellenic civilisations. You won't know it. Five years old: published by the University Press: better fetch me the Manager.'

I said: 'Do you mean *Early Minoan Cults* by James Fane?'

He said: 'That's it. That's it. Bring me a copy. Want a look at it. May not throw any light on ...' He murmured on for a bit without looking at me, but I recognised some phrases belonging to the chapter when Daddy was trying out the dictaphone and we all listened in to the records with great excitement. So I was able to say: 'I think it does. Chapter Five.' (Very proud.) He looked at me then. 'Know about ancient Greece?' I said no, but I knew that book, and the author's work.

'Do you, indeed? How's that?'

I explained, and he twitched his eyes and shook hands with me. Such glory! Everyone in the department was watching. (Though on second thoughts, they may just have thought he was my uncle.) Anyway, I gave him the bill, and he said: 'Good man that. Send me his next book.' Then he jerked the

PART I – AUTUMN

I never could draw dogs

bull terrier round and wandered off. Wasn't it nice? And I'm sure he was somebody of immense importance.

But no one actually knows. Speculation has been running high, as he's not one of our 'steadies'. Mr Salt can't remember ever having seen him before, though he's sure he's a 'familiar face in Cambridge'.

But where am I to send Daddy's next book, when written?

HILARY

BUSINESS AS USUAL

EVERYMAN'S STORES
For use in inter-departmental correspondence only

From M E Ward

To Mr Grant
October 21th, 1931

Subject Junior Assistant S (T) 801. Book Floor

Memo

I enclose Mr Salt's report on Miss Fane's work. She does not seem to be entirely justifying your confidence. I have spoken to her myself and pointed out that she must take her duties more seriously, and that it is impossible to over-estimate the importance of efficiency in detail. But I am not confident of having impressed her as I could wish. Miss Bryant actually found a drawing among her bills, which she very properly brought to me. Herewith.

BT/MEW

PART I – AUTUMN

EVERYMAN'S STORES
For use in inter-departmental correspondence only

From A Salt   *To* Miss Ward
                  October 21th

Subject Junior Assistant S (T) 801. Book Floor

Memo

Miss Fane has worked in the Book Department for a week. Her daily takings average £20. Manner with customers good. Shows great promise as a saleswoman, but Miss Bryant (Cash Desk) complains that her arithmetic is very poor. Six of her bills have been returned to her this week. Four required correction and two were illegible.

She needs constant supervision in this respect, and I have seen her counting on her fingers, which does not tend to inspire confidence in customers. Otherwise she has been satisfactory.

BT/MEW

BUSINESS AS USUAL

EVERYMAN'S STORES

For use in inter-departmental correspondence only

From M G Grant *To* Miss Ward

October 21th, 1931

Subject Junior Assistant S (T) 801. Book Floor

Memo

Try her in the library. Believe they add less there.

SN/MGG

PART I – AUTUMN

23 BURFORD STREET

October 23rd

MY DEAR,

They've moved me again. Into the Library this time, which means direct proximity to Miss Sparling and seems one of the less likely successes. Psychically our auras can't match or something. In effect, we like each other less and less.

I'm sorry to leave the 'Shop', too. When one wasn't being harried by bills and parcels and sales summaries it was an amusing place, and Mr Salt and I had begun to appreciate each other. I listened for half an hour yesterday to his views on *Let's Join the Nudists*. (Select nonfiction, 21/-, with eighteen photogravures, a signed photograph of the author, clad, and various bowery glimpses of him unclad, as the title had led one to hope.) Mr Salt holds rather progressive views, but I can't help feeling that he's one of the people who are better undenuded. Business doesn't develop the right muscles. As he says, 'it's the sitting that's the trouble'. And after beagles and the Cam, Paddington Recreation Ground hasn't much to offer a man.

I've listened to quite a lot of his reminiscent talk, one way and another, so when my transfer came he was good enough to tell me that I should be missed in the department, where, if he might say so, I had already made my mark. (Which is such a grand way of saying that I'd taken £112:5:6 in a week. I'd like to know, incidentally, how that compares with the takings of the child in the Inexpensive Gowns who gave me my first glimpse of sales technique in action.)

Well, I was sent to the Library yesterday, after a series of epic interviews with Miss Ward. I'm afraid she's disappointed in me. We don't see eye to eye over essentials. She thinks that Detail is Duty: Duty Detail ... Also that one cannot be efficient and draw faces in Sales books. It wastes paper and encourages levity in others.

As for Miss Sparling, she can hardly bear to explain things to me. She spent an hour elaborating the details of her system, all of which I forgot because she couldn't or wouldn't mention any underlying principle. Things, she told me, had always been done in a certain way, and therefore must always continue to be done just so. She may have had her reasons, but she refuses to part with them for my benefit. And I'm sure that's suspicious.

For instance, she told me that the folder for Mrs Jackson's library list must be marked R/R and Miss Graham's R/R − O ps/3. I said why? And she told me that there was a very good reason. When I said that I didn't doubt it but that I'd like to know, for my own edification what it was, she said that no department could be run without co-operation and that I was showing quite the wrong spirit.

After that she told me to take charge of one of the subsidiary desks, and showed me grimly where the folders were kept. From what Miss Ward said I gathered that I wasn't to be given a desk, but to spend my time learning the library system. It isn't entirely satisfactory and Mr Grant wants a report. But I expect Miss Sparling thought it would humble me to be given charge of Fiction C. It might, possibly, keep me out of mischief and prying. She gave me to understand that Fiction C was an extremely unimportant section, so that I would be likely to do less damage by making mistakes there than anywhere else.

The best people don't have Fiction C subscriptions, because they only cost 10/- a year and provide the copies that other people have spilt tea over or dropped in the bath. The titled or indolent send menials to Miss Rivington for Fiction A or to Miss Landry for A Select. All the A subscribers come under the Rational Reading scheme, but the Fiction C pariahs appear unobtrusively in person and carry their books away in leathercraft satchels or string bags.

I shall have to do my researches during the lunch hour, as I don't know whether Miss Sparling's underlings are well disposed. I think that they look on me (with reason) as a snake in the grass.

So much for me. How are you? I hear from the Family that all the pipes have burst at University Close, after a fortnight's trial by frost. Father has retired in dudgeon to a hotel to finish his book, but Mother is standing siege to set an example to the maids. What about Mrs MacQueen's pipes? Has she managed to nurse them through the convalescent stage, or are you angrily shaving in kettlefuls of hot water from your sitting-room fire? I pray that the frost doesn't migrate to London, or my basement will be uninhabitable. So far it's merely rained, which is hard on the one-pair-of-shoes girl, but not chilling to the bones.

Now, bed. I embark on semi-criminal investigations tomorrow. And if the truth must be told I'm feeling my position.

You may not get a letter till next week, because I'm going to the Bellamys' for the week-end, and you know dear Margaret and George think that if you're inactive for an instant you can't be having a good time. Not quite the weekend for a tired business girl. But who cares? Shall I give them your love?

  Anyway, mine herewith,

       HILARY

PART I – AUTUMN

Train

Sunday evening
October 25th

MY DEAREST FAMILY,

I'm writing this on the way back from the Bellamys. Margaret sent you her love. She and George hope to see you on their way north in the spring. They're going to motor through the Highlands and then tramp. As Margaret says, if she can't go to Nice she'll go to Cape Wrath instead. Better to be braced in Scotland than drenched on the English Riviera.

It was a very grand week-end. Perfectly glorious, I suppose, except for some of the usual moments. But if a two-figure income person goes to stay with four-figure friends, she may as well be philosophic and expect them.

I'd got the four figures rather on my mind, of course, in spite of theories, so I started preparations on Wednesday evening. I revived my better evening dress with half a bottle of benzine, and then took the other half to the evening shoes that had suffered from my last partner's feet. Only, I put them too near the gas fire afterwards, and while I was opening the door to let the petrol out, one shoe quietly went up in smoke. (Keep calm: there was no conflagration, and I didn't burn a finger-tip. But I was left with one shoe and a smoking puddle of ash.) That rather settled the economies. I took it as an omen and went shopping in the lunch hour. (When Staff Discount is allowed.) I bought a pair of evening shoes and stockings and a pair of pyjamas fit for the Bellamy corridors with the tail-end of my birthday money eked out with some of my deposit account. But I thought my bedroom slippers would just have to do, as a penance, though a mouse had rather eaten the fur in places.

When I arrived at Bath, the shining Bellamy car was there to meet me, and the chauffeur beside the ticket collector, touching his cap enquiringly to anyone who looked qualified to be a guest in the Bellamy household. I had an uneasy feeling that he was going to let me pass unchallenged, so I gave him my suit-case and swept out without waiting to see if he were surprised. But from that moment the question of tips (which usually only spoils the last afternoon in the houses of one's grander friends) worried me to distraction. Ought one in the circumstances, to tip the chauffeur by the piece as it were, instead of as a final gesture? I wished I'd asked you in my last letter as I'd meant to. I began to have wild ideas of stopping the car in the village and sending you a pre-paid wire. But then I remembered that the answer would probably come by telephone and be brought to me vocally by some menial in a very public place.

The Bellamys' house is five miles out of the village, on top of a hill, with a long avenue of noisy beech trees leading up to it. The outside is just ordinary country house-like and not particularly period or imposing. It's all in the plumbing: every bed its own bath in appropriately coloured tiles. Mine's green, with a sunk, jade-coloured pool and every conceivable cosmetic grouped round on glass shelves, and pale green, *enormous* bath towels warming on racks.

I wanted to stay safely in my room: Margaret and George were out. I thought I might unpack quickly and without any publicity that way. But Margaret's maid wouldn't have it: she shepherded me down to the music-room, and assured me that Madam would not be five minutes. The houseparty was playing in a golf tournament. It's a lovely room, of course; cream panelled, with old rose silks for cushions and curtains and a perilously parquet floor with Polar bear rugs. I find that sort of persistent beauty much more chastening than Aunt

Bertha's cheerful opulence. Anyway, I sat there, gradually deflating and turning over Society papers to complete the process, and ultimately then a young man in hairy tweeds whistled his way in. He looked rather disappointed at seeing me, I thought. But he said:

'Hallo. Did you win?'

I was disappointed too, because I hadn't thought it was going to be one of those weekends. It's so much more fun when you can get Margaret alone. I said, 'No,' and didn't explain till he asked if my partner had let me down. He said: 'No? Really? Then you're not the Smithers girl?'

I said, 'No,' and he said, 'No?' and just then Margaret and George came in. I think Margaret was really pleased to see me, but there were dozens of other tweeded, tramping people, all babbling about drives and bunkers and short putts. So it was difficult to be sure. I watched them all to hear who was called Smithers, hoping it might be the fair one with a coat and skirt rather like mine. But she turned out to be the plainish, spectacled creature who was there because the Female Celebrity never Moved without her secretary. Which rather crushed me. And in the middle of tea, the parlourmaid came in and spoke to Margaret. Margaret said: 'Hilary, darling – your keys. For Bates.' Everybody seemed to have stopped talking just then, and I daren't tell them that, having no valuables, I never locked my luggage. (In case they asked the reason.) So I handed over the muddle of half a dozen keys that all unlocked something irrelevant, and were tied together with very chewed string. They were borne off on a salver.

When I went up to change, my possessions were spread out and looking worse than usual. Bates had put out my new stockings with the 5/11 ticket face upwards: the mouse-bitten bedroom slippers were warming in front of the fire: all the oddments of pencil-sharpeners, bits of india rubber, pencils, hair-ribbon and farthings which always collect at the bottom of my case had been ranged neatly on the dressing-table among Margaret's shagreen brushes and mirrors and crystal bottles, and my two-shilling jar of cold cream. My very sponge-bag was marooned among flagons of bath-salts and vases of cologne and bowls of powder. By the time I'd bathed, though, I felt better, and after sherry I was quite pleased with myself. Dinner was lovely: odd, interesting things divinely cooked and served. The coffee I'd once spilt on my frock didn't really show, and if the first young man had thought I was like the spectacled Smithers the one sitting next to me seemed to find me amusing. So things were about even on Smithers.

I was rather haunted by the spectre of bridge towards the end, though. It took Daddy five years to teach me auction, as you know, and Basil couldn't teach me contract at all. Quite apart from the financial problem raised by their probable stakes.

But mercifully the Female Celebrity wanted to play paper games. I saw the unfortunate Smithers wince, and Margaret told me afterwards that the Celebrity made a point of outdoing everyone in vulgarity on those occasions. Last night she certainly succeeded. Smithers kept her head down over her own paper and got gradually purple about the ears, but she managed to win first Prize all the same. I thought that tactless, but apparently it was quite according to plan. She got a powder compact and the Female Celebrity carried off the Booby Prize; gold pencil and lipstick combined; three guineas at Everyman's, and probably five in Bond Street. I didn't think it of Margaret, but I suppose that if you have Celebrities to stay you can't stick at changing round the prizes where necessary.

Then we danced; a merciful change. People danced with me quite reasonably often and the floor was perfect. We went to bed just before two o'clock. (My sheets *and* blankets were the loveliest shade of new leaf green. Such fun.)

Breakfast appeared this morning about ten, with orange juice for the liver and complexion in a little glass jug. I thought I'd have it always, too. But on second thoughts it makes such a difference if other people can be hired to take out the pips and do the squeezing.

I came down about eleven, and Margaret said that she'd seen nothing of me at all and would I come with her in the car to inquire about a friend's new baby. It seemed that mere telephoning would be heartless, so we toured the hot houses, collected fruit and flowers, and drove about eighty miles, there and back, before lunch. I think that was the nicest bit of the week-end, for Margaret is such a darling, when she can be prised away from her great possessions.

After lunch some of us played tennis. Margaret lent me a racket and one of her dresses, which she insisted on my taking away afterwards. So I knew that I looked all right. Margaret's clothes are so lovely: she always makes me feel like a cow in a coat. But I played quite well. Not the grandest green rubber court in the world, of course, could help it being rather sad and autumnal. We had to keep moving all the time and wear gloves on our left hands. Yellow leaves flapped in the wire netting.

I'd only just got warm and begun to wish that I could go on staying when we had to go in to tea. We played again afterwards, but that set was spoiled because the tipping problem came down on me again like an extinguisher. Who, and how much, and when …? They beat us rather easily: 6-2.

Then after all, Margaret drove me to the station herself. So I just didn't tip that chauffeur. I don't suppose I shall be asked again, anyway.

On the whole, a lovely week-end. But the trouble about that sort of thing is that one should either do it so often that it gets to be a habit or not do it at all. I meant to tell you all about it, because I've been so rushed lately that my letters have been rather short and dull. But on re-reading I can think of lots of amusing things that I didn't tell you about. Only I must write gratefully to Margaret before I forget.

Keep having Basil to meals, won't you, even if he and Daddy do go polysyllabic in company. I don't believe that Mrs MacQueen feeds him properly. And he'd never notice.

With much love

HILARY

23 BURFORD STREET

October 29th

BASIL!

What did I tell you! I *knew* there was going to be trouble from my first day in the Library. And when the Minor Prophet gave me another complaint to investigate to-day I felt it was due. The details of the complaint aren't particularly significant, but actually a Rational Reader wrote from Northumberland (Mail Service, Provincial Branch) to protest. His first letter, written months ago, explained his requirements: a biography, a play and a first-class novel every month. His letter hadn't been acknowledged, and he continued to receive a succession of rubbishy novels – and battered copies at that.

Fiction C, obviously, poor man. Mr Grant passed the complaint to me, because Fiction C was my section. Would I kindly take the matter up? I could use his name as my authority for any investigations it might be necessary to make. I took the matter up with my knees knocking.

Have you ever tried to fix responsibility on anyone, Basil? It's about as easy as holding an unwilling frog in wet hands. I combed the Library, the Clerical Department, and the very Store Room to find that first missing, unacknowledged letter of September 30th. It took me two hours. In fact, it was more or less a case of:

Pig won't get over the Stile,

And I

Shan't get home to-night.

But finding it was worse. I went back to the Library, where Miss Sparling, of course, had never seen the thing in her life.

But I thought she looked rather hot and flummoxed, and she'd certainly just shut her Unwritten Letter Box when I arrived. Also, there was a blue letter scrunched up in the waste-paper basket.

'What's that?' I said (terrified).

'What's what?'

'That letter.'

'What letter?'

'In the waste-paper basket.'

'Of no importance, naturally. Otherwise, it wouldn't be there. Go back to your work.'

'I'm going to find that letter. I shall look in that basket.' (Very firm, but quaking).

'You'll do nothing of the sort '

We'd both raised our voices by then: she was raging like a cornered tabby. Mercifully it was lunch hour and there was nobody in the Library. I could just hear the lunch time music coming across the Lift Hall from the Restaurant. I was angry enough to tear the basket away from her by force, and I must have looked it. She's a wispy person. So she gave in. 'Very well. There's nothing of any consequence that I know of in that basket.' But she was blotchy with fright.

It was there, of course. I'd known, as if I'd seen her do it, that she'd found it just before I came in and been in too great a hurry to get rid of the piece of evidence that she knew I was looking for. Poor devil. She admitted to an 'Oversight.' But looked daggers.

And now I shall have to make a report, heaven help me. Oh, Basil, isn't losing your temper awful? Don't let's *ever* quarrel. I'm exhausted.

HILARY

EVERYMAN'S STORES

For use in inter-departmental correspondence only

From H Fane *To* Mr Grant
October 29th, 1931

Subject Rational Reading Service

Sub. L. Prov. 5196 (letter attached)

I   This complaint is the result of a general lack of method rather than of individual carelessness.

It is almost impossible to apportion the blame because no one will accept responsibility for a 'slight slip' – much less for a 'gross error'.

So far, it has been impossible to prove that the original instructions were received, and if they were not, the whole affair degenerates into an 'unfortunate mishap' for which no one can be blamed.

II   *Attempts to trace the letter.*

(a) *It is not in the Library.*
Miss Sparling says she can never have had it, as she never forgets a distinctive hand, especially on blue paper.

(b) *There is no sign of it in the Files.*
Miss Lamb says she rather thinks she may have seen a letter something like it, but if she had she wouldn't dream of sending it to file, and it an incomplete order. She hopes she is giving satisfaction, and she is sure she is very careful over her work. If anyone makes a slight slip and sends an unanswered letter to file, she always points it out to them.

(c) *It is not in the Mail Order Despatch.*
Mr Simpson, who handles these orders, thinks he saw it, but if so, he must have passed it on to Mr Millet. Otherwise, the books the gentleman ordered would have gone. He is a very conscientious man with a life-long experience of mail orders.

(d) *It is not in the Book Store.*
Mr Millet says he is sure he saw it. He remembers the notepaper, and the name of one of the books: it was out of stock, so he passed the order to Miss Watts for a letter.

(e) *It is not in the Clerical Department.*
Miss Watts remembers nothing about it. If an order was given to her to acknowledge, she would have acknowledged it, that is, if it were part of her work. But library queries are not part of her work. If she had such a thing, she would have got rid of it at once, by querying it with Miss Hopper.

(f) *It is not with Miss Hopper.*
Miss Hopper says there is something familiar about the letter, but she can't be sure. But if a slip has been made it is not her fault. She might have passed a letter rather like this one to Miss Sparling, because she cannot enter anything on her index without Miss Sparling has had it first and initialled it in red. It's against the regulations.

(g) Further search only produced more disclaimers, a great deal of dust, several packets of bull's eyes, some chocolate that had been overlooked, a *Home Chat*, and a *Daily Mail* for 1929 and 1930 respectively. These have now been destroyed.

III   *Conclusion.*

It is difficult to estimate the reliability of these rumours about a blue letter passed through the department and left no trace. Probably several people thought they had seen it just to be on the safe side. I believe that proper records could easily be organised to prevent future mistakes, but my experience of the Library and the Rational Reading Services is too short for me to make recommendations of much value. I should say, however, that the whole system suffers from lack of method, and possibly also from lack of imagination on the part of those who chose the books for the de luxe services.

H FANE

2.30 pm   In continuation of the above memo. The letter of September 30th has now been found in the Library waste-paper basket. I have repaired it and attached it herewith. It had apparently been overlooked – in spite of the distinctive hand-writing.

H F

EVERYMAN'S STORES

For use in inter-departmental correspondence only

From M G Grant *To* Miss Fane
October 30th, 1931

Subject Your memo of yesterday's date

Good. I should like you to remain on the Book Floor for the present, to investigate the system on which the Library and the Rational Reading Services are run, and if necessary, to supervise the introduction of improvements such as you indicate.

Please see me about this at 12.15 to-day.

M G G

SN/MGG

23 BURFORD STREET

October 30th, 1931

DARLING,

Life is too much for me. I've brought off the sleuthing triumphantly and been thanked by the Minor Prophet, and told that I may consider my appointment to the Library confirmed – with a hint of promotion to follow.

But I don't think that I can bear it. Miss Sparling now loathes me so that it obviously hurts her to pass me on the stairs and her underlings loathe me in proportion. The whole place is vile with intrigue and corner-conversations that stop when I come past. I thought this sort of atmosphere was only found in girls' boarding schools. It seems to belong to business as well. I'd no idea what devils women could be to other women in an entirely passive way, and I've never wanted to talk to you so much in my life. Just to hear you say, 'My dear child, what *does* it all matter?' (in the way that I don't always like) would make all the difference now. I've been saying it to myself all the way home in the bus, but the charm won't work for me.

I got home late to-night and it was raining, and I've got a cold and my basement looked just too cheerless. Mrs Hemming had left the wastepaper basket uncleared and I hadn't enough pennies for the gas. I sat on the edge of the bed and cried, because I had a cold and made the cold worse by crying. Then I looked round the basement and thought of the house in University Close and the way it would welcome me. Why should I try to be grand and earn my living among Sparlings, and live in a basement just to carve out a career?

What's the use of being noble and obstinate and uncomfortable? I shall tell Mr Grant tomorrow that I'm not the creature he thought I was, and that I can't bear it any longer and will he let me go away with my tail between my legs.

You were right. Everybody was right. And I was wrong. You said that I couldn't stand the hours and that I'd give it up in a month. I'm a weakling and a worm, and I wonder if I can get off in time to catch the train from St Pancras to-morrow night. Just think of being in Scotland in time for breakfast! Will you be good enough not to say 'I told you so?' Not that that'll matter, since you'll obviously be thinking it for days. I'm ashamed of myself. I'm dreadfully ashamed of myself, but I'm so *miserable* that it doesn't seem to make any difference. The sawdust's out of me.

HILARY

31st October

Hilary to Basil

Telegram

Basil Rainford Christophers Hospital Edinburgh

Cancel letter posted last night deil take the hindmost staying on.

HILARY

Part II – Winter

EVERYMAN'S STORES

For use in inter-departmental correspondence only

From M G Grant   *To* Miss Fane
November 3rd, 1931

Subject

Personal

It occurred to me after our recent discussion that you were not altogether happy at the thought of further work in the Library.

I should like to take the opportunity of assuring you that I would not make the arrangement which I have in mind without being quite sure that you can, if you will, do work there which will be of real service to the firm.

                                           M G GRANT

SN/MGG

November 3rd

MY DEAR,

Why shouldn't I change my mind? That isn't a truculent question: I'm quite good-tempered, but really anxious to know. Friday's stupid letter was written in one of those impulses – you know what an outcry I always make in the fell clutch of circumstance. It oughtn't to have been taken any more seriously than the ravings of any other temporarily irresponsible creature. Especially when I went to the trouble of recanting next morning at the cost of one and fivepence.

I thought that wire might amuse you. But you were furious. Why? Because, as you said, it was all a childish business to begin with and especially when I had those outbreaks and sent contradictory messages by following posts? Or was it because you wanted me to fail all the time that my telegram ruffled you? Or because you wanted to see me and were disappointed that I wasn't coming home after all? I hope it was the last reason, but I can't help feeling that if it had been you'd have found an excuse that'd have held enough water to bring you to London at least once during the last two months. So it looks rather as if it weren't that.

But whatever the reason was, don't you really think it'd have been ignoble to come crawling home? It wouldn't have meant that I'd 'seen reason at last', but only that I'd been whipped. And I'd never have been able to forget that:

> This little pig went squealing
>
> *All* the way home …

Besides, if one's been told by anybody who knows that one's going to do 'work of real importance to the firm', it ought to be exciting to stay and see if that's true. Don't you agree?

Of *course* it's nothing to do with us. And of course it doesn't mean that I've 'lost my sense of proportion so completely as to be blind to real obligations'. Why should it mean anything so grand-sounding and silly? You knew when I came up that I meant to work for a year. And I still mean to (with lapses). It's quite evident that, as you say, you've been saving up for an opportunity to put your views before me. And now that you've spread out all the evidence against me I don't know that I like the look of it much. Do you really think things out as thoroughly as that always? Do you let grievances pile themselves up, I mean, like cards in a card-index till the moment arrives to catalogue them? I'd feel so much safer if you merely clouted me occasionally.

However, if you like things to be set out neatly you might as well have my tabulated replies.

Kindly note that:

(1) I am in receipt of your instructions.

(2) I don't like them.

(3) I'm not coming home just yet.

(4) I repudiate the expression 'tomfoolery' as applied to my present work.

(5) I consider that you have been:

    (a) Churlish.

    (b) Rude.

    (c) Entirely obtuse.

                  Yours faithfully,

                    HILARY FANE
                    Librarian

23 BURFORD STREET

November 4th

MY POOR DEARS,

After twenty-eight years of me you ought really to recognise my 'Wolf, wolf!' bleat when you hear it, but I'm sorry to have given you such an anxious day.

What happened was this: they promoted me, rather without warning, and I thought it was going to be quite unbearable. Nothing but hurt feelings, black looks and savage little rows – all the time. The atmosphere was electric: I felt like a galvanised frog. Afterwards I wrote to Basil in a panic. I'm very ashamed, as I thought I'd changed my mind in time to prevent the clamour from reaching you.

It was all a very stupid fuss, and I feel better now. I had a long talk with Mr Grant. He's the firm's Organising Director, and rather over my (clerk's) horizon, so you haven't heard of him before. But he's an enthusiast, with broods and broods of reforms, and I'm to foster one of them. It's to be quite a position – not just a job. (I can hardly wait till Friday to see if there's any recognition of the change in my pay envelope.)

We had an odd interview. Miss Ward (Staff Supervisor, and one of those large, Gorgon women) had unfortunately found a drawing of mine in my Sales Book and taken it to Mr Grant in the best tradition. He pulled it out of a drawer just as I was going away and handed it to me with: 'Dangerous likeness. Draw the customers at home.' (Do you remember the weekend when you came to fetch me home from school and were greeted by the news that I'd caricatured the Head and was in the Sick Room till Monday? How people's methods vary.)

Honestly, though, you needn't worry. The Library's a revelation after the tomes and people of the municipal establishment. It's a marvellous place, rather like the Zoo in a nightmare, because one's so apt to feed the lions with literary sprats and the pelicans with horse flesh. So far, subscribers seem to divide up into those who insist on choosing their own books in order to curse the authors, and the others who prefer to leave the choice to us so that they can curse the Librarians. Other people, stranded in the grimmer suburbs, keep sending us lists of dead and moribund authors and demanding their latest books. So you see I'm all right, swelling with forbidden laughter, but exuding the requisite tact.

Much love,

HILARY

BUSINESS AS USUAL

23 BURFORD STREET

November 6th

MY DEAREST FAMILY,

I *like* being an official investigator, on second thoughts. I've received instructions to look into the Library system, trace up the complaints, and evolve any necessary modifications likely to check them. So I've been quite definitely a person to placate. And numbers of innocent but apprehensive people keep coming up to me and saying how lucky I am to have a natural wave, and can they lend me things. My arch-enemy, however, who reigns there, has remained aloof without offering me the merest hairpin. I accept all attentions calmly, but they're very good for the inferiority complex.

In my new capacity I've just spent the morning in our Filing Vault, checking up outcries from subscribers. Everyman's filing system is stupendous, of course. An immense room is full of filing cabinets and sorting tables and short step-ladders and clothes-baskets spilling with letters and people in pinafores are busy among the electric light fans and telephones and dangling, humanely green-shaded lights.

Because, you see, every communication, every letter, telegram or picture post card that anybody ever sends us is stamped with the customer's number and index letters as soon as it comes into the building: it finds its way to the Vault, with a copy of our reply as soon as it's been answered. Then it's filed for reference, with carbons of all invoices made out against that customer, for two years (and probably a day). After which it's torn up.

So when I'd collected a bunch of typical grumbles the first thing to do was to look up the history of the grumblers in the Vault. (Occasional complainers, of course, receive preferential treatment to the habitual ones.) But the first thing I did in the Vault was to take out the correspondence of all the people I knew who dealt with Everyman's – just out of sheer, furious female curiosity. It was rather a shattering experience. There they all were; nice, harmless, amusing people, giving presents with one hand and writing long, passionate letters about postal overcharges with the other.

Aren't people odd? What *happens* to them the instant money leaves their hands? Sell your best friend a packet of biscuits or a toothbrush or a silk handkerchief or a library subscription, and the most angelic personality is immediately submerged by the obsession of Getting one's Money's Worth. I didn't read through many files: it was too indecent. I went quickly on to my pile of letters from fulminating Colonels in Bedford and Bath and Harrogate who complain that they got nothing but 'pert novels by pups', and the women who are 'quite at a loss to understand …'

I've made a rough record, and to-morrow I shall have to present it, suitably modified, to Authority as represented by Mr Grant, who also expects me to suggest remedies. But this afternoon I shall just meekly supervise Fiction C and plan campaign.

With my love,

HILARY

From Hilary Fane's notebook

COMPLAINTS

These seem to resolve themselves into three groups:

(1) *Personal vociferation in the Library,* with which this investigation is happily not at present concerned.

(2) *By telephone.* Have encountered various.

    (a) (Piteous.) 'Is there *no one* in this building who understands …'

    (b) (Truculent.) You are the seventh young woman to whom I have explained my requirements …'

    (c) (Involved.) 'One of your assistants – the name escapes me – sold me a book on bees to be sent to a friend in Spain, and charged to my brother in Scotland. I went straight home and sent you the corrected address – on a post card, I fancy – but the book has not yet arrived. Can you explain?'

(3) *By letter.* May be subdivided as follows:

    (i) From suburban subscribers, usually written in pencil on the back of one of firm's worse-typed letters, and frequently illegible.

    (ii) From subscribers with measles or something equally microbial, who do not see why they should be prevented from returning library books in the usual way.

    (iii.) From subscribers variously disappointed with the

Mail Provincial Subscriptions run in connection with Rational Reading or Rational Reading de Luxe Services.

NB – Find with reference to these, that subscribers in a fine heat of indignation almost invariably understamp letters. One communication reads: 'I am sending this bill back to you unstamped to teach you not to pester me with such things again.'

Preliminary Record

Subscriber	*Complaint*	*Comment or Suggestion*
R/R de Luxe Sub. 4532 (Canterbury)	Ordered THE SUEZ CANAL AND ITS TRAFFIC PROBLEMS. Received CLEARING THE ALIMENTARY CANAL.	Recommend more careful use of digestive treatises in future.
R/R Branch Service Sub. 4567 (Ascot)	'Why don't you send the book I ask for: ACCIDENT IN A HOTEL by Baum?'	Have sent all works of this author, seriatim.

Fiction A. Delivery 6 Sub. 8945 (Harrow)	'Where are my library books? I wrote three times last week. Still no books. Surely a firm of your standing …'	Exhaustive inquiry has produced three post cards. (a) Unsigned (b) Without titles (c) Quite blank
R/R Non-Fiction A. Fiction B. Prov. Sub. 4452 (Godalming)	'Kindly note. I *will not have:* Books by Women. Books on sex. First novels. Short Stories. Realism or Morbidity. Travel or Biography. Essays.	Return his money
R/R Prov. Non-Fiction A. Sub 5768 (Cheltenham)	'Have subscribed to your library for six months and made my wishes abundantly clear to anyone with modicum of intelligence. But have received consistent stream of trash. Consider SHAKEDOWN absolutely beyond the pail (sic.).	Curry-gutted Anglo-Indian Soothe

Note – Find 'Assistant's oversight' had been regretted in all cases. Do not consider this elastic phrase altogether happy and recommend variety.

BUSINESS AS USUAL

November 10th

DARLING,

I was thankful to find your letter waiting for me this evening. Last week has been abominable. In another two days I should have broken out into abject apologies. But your forgiveness arrived in time to save my face. So now I can say how really sorry I am about that last letter of mine. Considering provocation, you've shown enough forbearance to make me feel a worm and not enough to make me turn on you.

Letters *are* difficult though, don't you think? I didn't realise how mine would read, next morning, over Mrs MacQueen's tea and kippers and blackened toast. And I'm sure that if you were here I could explain, and you would see why I've got to stay. Because you don't quite, even now. I suppose it sounds unlikely that one should begin to count in a firm of this size after two months. But I think it's true. Anyway, they've raised my salary. Isn't that fairly convincing?

My pay envelope had FOUR POUNDS in it last week. The extra notes were wrapped round a card, With The Compliments of the Management. So I'm not a clerk any longer. I'm a Business Woman. Unfortunately for my Budget, I brought neither of the extra notes home. I didn't touch my basic £2:10:0 (I have a conscience), but I bought a hat in one of the unfashionable shops that stay open till seven o'clock, a flask of eau-de-cologne, and fifty wickedly expensive Turkish cigarettes. I put my new hat on in the shop and dropped the old one into a perfect stranger's dustbin. Then I felt better, so I had dinner at the Criterion and went on to an Upper Circle, spending sixpence at Piccadilly Circus Underground telephoning various ex-Oxford people who were all too startled and poor to come with me.

And I was so overpowered by affluence that I slept in this morning and had to take a taxi to work. Which means dipping into the Emergency Fund. I've always distrusted Sudden Riches.

And it also means that for the rest of the week I shall have to lunch on one and threepence and have No Tea. Which is sure to larn me. Especially this weather. I always have a halfcrown hunger in an east wind. And there's one at present that seems to strip the clothes from your body and the flesh from your bones.

But it's fun to play Spartan for a week, knowing that four pounds will come to the rescue on Friday. I punched an extra hole in my belt to-day with nail scissors, and went about feeling like an hour-glass. But I doubt whether it's a practical expedient. My stomach got pins and needles in the middle of the morning, and I had to let myself out.

Heroically yours,

HILARY

EVERYMAN'S STORES

For use in inter-departmental correspondence only

From Staff Supervisor   *To* Miss Fane
                                            November 10th, 1931

Subject

Confidential

With reference to your appointment to the library (Fiction C) kindly note that this cancels your status as Junior Assistant S (T) 801. It will not be necessary for you to be given a library number in your new and more official capacity. Sister Smith will arrange accommodation for you in the Senior Staff Cloakroom. You will also have the privilege of entering by the West Door and of using the Lifts. (Except during the rush hours.)

I am sure you will appreciate that this position carries with it an added responsibility, not to be lightly assumed. I understand that you have Mr Grant's authority to make a certain number of investigations, and I shall always be ready to give advice where necessary. You will, of course, realise the need for tact and moderation when introducing innovations likely to affect persons of longer standing in the Department than yourself.

                                                    M E WARD

November 12th

REALLY BASIL,

How you and Miss Ward distrust me! She copes with me gingerly as if I were a bomb without a safety catch, and you say in effect that I ought never to have been promoted, because people are bound to resent it.

Actually, I'd thought of that for myself. Of course they would resent me, the people who had been clerks or typists for a dozen years and are going to be the same sort of underling for another twenty, unless they've saved enough money from a three-pound wage to buy themselves a little hat shop or one of those parrot-painted restaurants where they manage to give business girls lunch for one and six with coffee extra.

Of course, they were going to resent my being picked out and given the extra thirty shillings a week that would have brought the tea shop so much nearer. There wouldn't be any reason for the change as far as they could see: I typed worse than any of them, my labels weren't legible, I knocked books off tables and made my bills out wrong. How could they see the justice of picking out anyone for promotion just because of some nebulous quality that they had never had or that had been beaten out of them long ago? They wouldn't think it important that somebody anxious for responsibility should be in a position to take it (though later it might be very useful to be able to slide the responsibility for a misguided decision on to somebody else's shoulders). They wouldn't recognise that sort of ability. But they'd be bound to notice the messy typing and incorrect bills and things. They *show* so. And they'd put all the obvious things together and total Favouritism. That word would hiss round and round the Book Floor, only just out of my hearing. Oh, I knew. I'd been through it before.

So I was frightened, though I couldn't let anybody – not even you, for some reason or other – know it.

And the first day *was* unpleasant. I sat behind Fiction C's desk most of the time, and walked forbiddingly about, when I felt it necessary to show that I wasn't even aware of other people's eyes. I went into the Book Store and asked questions, and into the Clerical Department and asked more questions, and wrote the answers on little slips of paper which I was terrified of leaving about and which I usually lost through sheer panic. Then I stopped in the Shop to speak to Mr Salt. He was sympathetic, but cautious, so I guessed that he'd been hearing things about me. Obviously nothing would persuade him to discuss books with my sort of be-ribboned pi-dog any more.

But, since that first day, they've been very good to me. Miss Dowland and I still have tea together: Miss Hopper told me this morning that Miss Pim isn't half such a quick writer as I was, and Mr Simpson comes into the library specially to tell me about the re-binding of my very worst Fiction Cs, and stays beside my desk, staring into the distance, and talking about the sort of novels that people really like. 'Nothing too psychological,' he thinks (meaning sex). But I disagree. Fiction C adores sex. Suitably beglamoured.

Mr Millet draws me into the Book Store and tells me how many little matters we must look into together, and how, in his opinion, various things (and people) require expediting. If we could see eye to eye we might make a clean sweep. And after all, two heads are better than one, as they say.

Miss Sparling, of course, is permanently hostile. But I think that's more constitutional than anything else. She has one of those *painful* smiles at the best of times and even with our most influential subscribers.

Anyway, there are only one and a half more working days, and I've promised myself a Sunday out of London. Early breakfast, a packet of sandwiches, and a Metro train as far as it'll take me.

I might ring up various people and get them to come too, but I don't think I feel like company. When you work in a firm of fifteen hundred it's a new idea to be alone. If you were here it would be different. But I just don't feel promiscuous.

H

BURFORD STREET

Saturday evening
November 15th

DEAR BASIL,

I came in half an hour ago, just as it was getting dark. I've walked all day: I'm full of bread and cheese, and country air and blown out with pride at having done something that was good for me as well as being fun. It was one of our kind of walks, but unfortunately not to be followed by one of Mrs MacQueen's high teas. And I'd like one more than I can conveniently say.

The trouble about London, of course, is that it lasts so long, and even when one's twenty miles from Piccadilly Circus (or wherever they start the tape-measure) you find those SevenHundred-Pound Palaces festering all over perfectly good fields. But there was a west wind and a lovely curve of ploughed hillside against a pale sky, and the common I finally reached was purple and bronze and green with bracken and brambles. The sun came out as I was eating that bread and cheese in a circumspect little clearing among the bracken and silver birches. But even there the people were nearly as prevalent as the villas. Three gangs passed me: you know the type – sticks and mackintoshes and broad, sedentary beams, walking to whistles blown by young men with pink spots.

They passed me at full tilt, but later a youth who looked like Christian before the bundle fell off came up, and asked me if I could direct him. I said, 'What to?' And he said, 'The Windmill Inn'. So I told him, thinking it was because of beer, that I'd seen an inn of sorts at the edge of the common. Was I sure it was the Windmill. No, not a bit, but did it matter? He said it was vital, and did you pass a pond on the way to it?

I didn't think so, but I told him that there were lots of ponds, and did it have to be a special one? He said yes, and I said why and he explained that it was Marked in his Diagram.

So I rose to the occasion and said (quite recklessly) that he must bear half-right and then left, and then half-right again at the blasted beech stump. And he did. I choked down my last bite and hurried off, in case he should work out my directions backwards and arrive to complain. Then I went and had a cigarette on quite a different part of the common, and walked back to the station.

The station reminds me: when I got into the train at Baker Street this morning I saw Mr Salt, of all people, fidgeting on the platform, looking odd without his celluloid collar. He had reverted to type and was wearing incredibly dirty flannel bags, with a comparatively

141

respectable brown tweed coat and drastically striped tie. Of course I hung out of the window till the last minute to see who would arrive. And it was Miss Lamb! It's startling, somehow, to think of Mr Salt as Miss Lamb's Boy. They looked a little surprised at sight of each other, I thought. Miss Lamb was very grand but rather unfortunate in *her* dearest clothes, which were definitely high-heeled and urban. But they went off together rather obviously hoping for the best.

They can't have been out in the country before, in spite of the car that Miss Lamb was going to be allowed to drive when the summer came. What has he done with that car, anyway? And why Baker Street Station? Cheap day ticket, I expect. So much less exacting than sedentary amusements.

Six weeks till Christmas. Or is it seven? Shall I get longer leave now I'm so grand? Or none?

I love you,

HILARY

BURFORD STREET

November 16th

BASIL DARLING,

Such disgrace! My relations have let me down.

You remember my dear Aunt Bertha, who took us to eat unseasonable things at the Carlton in my last Trinity term? She beamed on you and said surely there wasn't much money in science, but everybody did do such odd things nowadays, didn't they?

Well, I might have guessed that she'd be a Rational Reader de Luxe. (A. Fiction and A. Select, six books at a time.) And I did know that yesterday was Remnant Day in all Depts. Poor Aunt Bertha! Neither a pork pie title nor ranks of lackeys can keep her from plunging passionately into the Sales. I ought to have expected her.

I suppose she'd spent a happy afternoon in the Soft Furnishings, trying to pick up some dragoned chintzes for chair covers at one and eleven-three or something equally impossible. Then, of course, fate must arrange for her to think of tea. And in the lift, it would occur to her to pop into the Library and tell the girl just what she thought of the latest de luxe books: not what she calls good reading – nasty things, so thin, and such wide margins, and those wood-cuts! So peculiar! Nothing in the world to do with the story as far as one can see. (Darling Aunt Bertha buys books by the barrel, and wouldn't really mind what we sent her as long as there were plenty of it for the money.)

If I'd been in retreat as usual, doing Fiction C, I might have escaped, but I'd just gone to help Miss Landry when Aunt Bertha exploded through the swing doors. She bore down on

A. Select, flung her books on the desk, tugged her hat over one ear, pushed her furs off her shoulder and began her piece. Then she recognised me. The desk was between us, but that didn't stop her.

Her arms, furs, plumes were all round me instantly. The whole room echoed with my name. (Platforms have made Aunt Bertha so devastatingly audible.) She said: how quaint of me to serve in a shop; and wasn't it amusing to find that I was the gel who sent her those dreadful books; and why – *why* was I doing it and did my Mother not know? I said 'Hush,' and 'Yes,' and 'Wasn't it,' and made faces, and tried to disentangle myself. But nothing stopped her.

'HER ARMS, FURS, PLUMES WERE ALL AROUND ME.'

Finally, she pulled me out, more or less by the scruff of the neck, tucked my hand under her arm, and announced that we would go and have a cup of tea. 'Where we can talk quietly,' she said, looking round the quite obviously enthralled spectators like Marie Antoinette from a tumbril. My dear, I absolutely ran her down the library. If tea would stop her, she should have it, even if I had to have it with her. Besides, I thought that no one knew me in the Restaurant, and *anything* to get her out of the Library, away from Sparling who seemed likely to have apoplexy behind her Michaelmas daisies.

I sat and listened to Aunt Bertha for forty-five minutes. She ordered muffins and went on to cream buns – because, as she says, if you are a little addicted to adiposity, you'd better eat what takes your fancy and be happy. She is, too. Both, bless her!

But of course we were in full view of the door by the Lifts, and I doubt if any creature in the Library, the Clerical Department, or the 'Shop' failed to find an errand to take him (or her) past it. The glass panes were so misted by their incredulous breathing that Mr Simpson had to wipe an eye-hole before he could locate me.

I never realised before quite what a Public Woman Aunt Bertha is. But since Uncle Tom was made a knight, she is in the public eye more or less continuously. Opening things, you know, and breaking bottles over liners. Quite one of Everyman's star customers, in fact. What Miss Sparling would call a 'familiar figure'.

So what with one thing and what with another, and food and guarded explanations and sociability it was more than three-quarters of an hour before I crawled back to Fiction C feeling rather bloated and longing for sleep, like a snake that's overeaten itself and would like to cast a skin. Miss Sparling looked at the clock, her watch and me as I came in; then she went on writing something so furiously that her pen spat.

When six o'clock eventually struck I was in such a bad temper that I just sat there for five unnecessary minutes clearing up to spite myself. Then I prodded my way out and climbed crossly on to a bus and sat down beside Mary Meldon.

You remember Mary? She used to live two doors away from us in University Close, and we've always been friendly. We've each known the other was in London for months, but in spite of all modern inventions we've lived within a ten minutes' bus ride and never been able to get into touch. As one does. So to-night, when I plumped down beside her we were both as startled as if the other had returned from somewhere as proverbially remote as Timbuctoo. But we were both very pleased with each other, and I took her and a pound of sausages home to supper. We thought that we'd go to a theatre afterwards, but our respective nine-to-sixes had left us both too exhausted to bear the idea of moving the body or exercising the brain any more.

So we sat and fed my gas fire to capacity with pennies and told each other the stories of our lives instead. It was such a success that we've arranged to do it again whenever life becomes overbearing.

I feel so cheered now that I could go on writing for hours. Except that nine o'clock next morning tends to drive one to bed by midnight.

And it's that now. Good-night, my lamb.

HILARY

EVERYMAN'S STORES

For use in inter-departmental correspondence only

From Miss Sparling. Library *To* Miss Ward

November 16th, 1931

Subject Miss Fane

Memo

I have been charge of the Library for six years, and I hope I have given satisfaction. In the interests of the Firm, therefore, I feel I ought to point out that the appointment of Miss Fane can only cause trouble. No amateur can be expected to deal with such complicated and specialised work after a few week's experience and no training whatever!

In my opinion at least, she is quite incompetent and a thoroughly bad influence for the other girls. She seems to enjoy making herself conspicuous, and this afternoon she so far forgot herself as to persuade one of our most important customers, Lady Barnley, to take her out to tea in the Restaurant, where she stayed twenty minutes beyond her regulation half-hour for tea.

I should just like to say that I cannot hold myself responsible for *anything* that occurs in the Library while Miss Fane is in it, which is most unfair to the other girls.

A G SPARLING

EVERYMAN'S STORES

For use in inter-departmental correspondence only

From Miss Ward *To* Mr Grant
November 16th, 1931

Subject Miss Fane. Library Assistant. Fiction C

Memo

I am sorry to trouble you again about Miss Fane, but her appointment to the Library seems to have caused more disturbance than I anticipated.

She has thoroughly upset Miss Sparling, who complains that she is unsettling the Library girls. Among other things, she prevailed upon one of our most important customers, Lady Barnley, to take her to tea in the Restaurant, where she stayed twenty minutes over her tea half-hour. I understand from Miss Fane that Lady Barnley is her aunt, but even allowing for the relationship, such conduct, as I have pointed out to her, was in very bad taste.

Perhaps you would like to speak to her yourself on this occasion.

M E WARD

BT/MEW

EVERYMAN'S STORES

For use in inter-departmental correspondence only

From M G Grant *To* Staff Supervisor

November 17th, 1931

Subject Miss Fane

Memo

I am not disposed to view this affair too seriously. At worst, it is a tiresome indiscretion. For your guidance in replying to Miss Sparling, I should perhaps mention that it has always been understood that the half-hour for tea allowed to members of the staff is at their own disposal. The majority prefer to take it in the canteen, but there is no regulation to prevent an assistant being taken out to tea in any public place by a relation, though the necessity for a punctual return might be pointed out to Miss Fane.

Further, Lady Barnley is, as we know by experience, easily offended. It might have been difficult had Miss Fane refused.

Miss Pane's appointment to the Library will not, of course, be affected by this, on the whole, irrelevant occurrence.

M G GRANT

SN/MGG

BUSINESS AS USUAL

EVERYMAN'S STORES
For use in inter-departmental correspondence only

From Staff Supervisor

To Miss Sparling
November 17th, 1931

Subject Miss H. Fane, Library Assistant

Memo

While appreciating your point of view in this matter, I am asked by Mr Grant to inform you that no regulation has actually been infringed by Miss Fane, though the usual fine will be levied in respect of the twenty minutes over-time taken for tea.

Her position in the Library will, therefore, be unaffected by the incident.

M E WARD

BT/MEW

EVERYMAN'S STORES

For use in inter-departmental correspondence only

From H Fane *To* Mr Grant
November 17th, 1931

Subject Personal

Memo

I am most frightfully sorry. If I had realised:

> Miss Sparling's sensations at the Incident
>
> Her rendering of it
>
> Miss Ward's reactions
>
> Your probable exasperation at this woman's wasp-nest
>
> And the interruption of Departmental Routine,

Nothing would have persuaded me to have tea with Aunt Bertha. And I assure you that my own feelings while providing a Roman Holiday for the Book Floor Staff were in themselves some penance. But I am willing to perform any other you may see fit to impose.

HILARY FANE

EVERYMAN'S STORES

For use in inter-departmental correspondence only

From M G Grant *To* Miss Fane
November 18th, 1931

Subject Your memo of yesterday's date

Memo. Personal

Quite. But no more bread and circuses.

M G G

SN/MGG

23 BURFORD STREET

November 18th

DEAREST MUMMY AND DADDY,

The mountain has fallen upon Mahomet! In other words, it's one thing for me to decide not to visit Aunt Bertha in her grandeur, and quite another (and impossible) for me to prophesy or prevent her visiting the Library in Everyman's, and recognising me.

It caused rather a sensation, I'm afraid: I had to make my peace with the authorities afterwards. And also to go to lunch with Aunt Bertha and explain very elaborately why it would be better for those family reunions to take place in private.

It was a very amusing luncheon party. Just the two of us. Uncle Tom was away. Aunt Bertha adored hearing as much about Everyman's as I thought safe to tell her, considering all her presidential connections with Welfare Societies and Boards. My own career, she says, will have her special attention. I only hope she won't wreck it. Aunt Bertha's such a haphazard guardian angel – *so* apt to trouble the waters!

But she gave me a superb, enormous meal and insisted on my drinking rather a lot of burgundy, because it was 'so blood-making'. All this in her palatial club, as it would have been beyond me to reach Cadogan Square, eat a meal and be back in Everyman's within an hour. And I've already mortgaged my 'shopping hour' for November. As it was, we discovered over coffee that I had three minutes in which to get back to the Book Floor. This, in Charles Street, aristocratically inaccessible by bus! I shot up, murmuring about taxis and trying to remember whether my bag had two shillings and a halfpenny or two half-pennies and a shilling in it. But Aunt Bertha took charge of the situation, beaming.

'I thought this might happen,' she said. 'So I told Edwards to wait. I know what it is to be a woman of many engagements.' (Rather an exalted description of my activities, on the whole.) So I was borne, slightly comatose, up to the very Staff Entrance of Everyman's, in an enormous, dove-grey, appallingly conspicuous Hispano-Suiza. I'd meant to tell Edwards to put me down at the corner, but the burgundy made the extra exertion of reaching for the speaking-tube unthinkable. Also, between Fanes, it's not every day that I have the chance of such an opulent return from lunch. But there were disappointingly few people about. The two shillings fortunately proved to be a half-crown, which I stoically gave to Edwards. I shall lunch on tick to-morrow … and to-morrow.

Aunt Bertha sent all sorts of messages to you both, and then, finally, said that she would write herself. So you'll probably be amused.

Rumours of the Christmas Rush are rolling about already. As Christmas Day falls, mercifully, on a Friday, I ought to get away on Thursday night and have three clear days at home. I might even be able to get an extra concession because of my long journey. I'll try and find out. Lovely to be back again. I wonder what leave Basil will get. That probably depends on your own conscience, though, when you're as grand as he is, and that's always so uncomfortable. Anyway, I'll take every minute I can wring out of the management. Appalling to remember the fourteen weeks' vacs that I thought nothing of in the Oxford days. Now a long week-end seems munificence.

This week-end I'm going to spend with the Meldons (who used to live next door but two in University Close). I'm expecting to enjoy it more than the Bellamys. The Meldons are poor but nice: like us.

With lots of love,

HILARY

BURFORD STREET

November 19th

MY DEAR,

I agree. It *was* one of those women's fusses about next to nothing, and I'm thankful to say that nothing much seems to be coming of it. But Sparling still goes about like one of those ancestral voices prophesying war.

I've done my best. I apologised to Authority and went to lunch with Aunt Bertha, and implored her not to call for me personally in the Library. I pointed out that people who were above such merely mortal emotions as jealousy might like me to have grand relations for the sake of the shop's prestige. But people like Sparling couldn't really be expected to enjoy seeing their latest interloper fêted by their special celebrities. Aunt Bertha quite understood that. I left her flattered, and conspiratorially promising me the cold shoulder for as long as I required it. 'So romantic; quite a little kingdom of its own! I shall tell the Federated Women Citizens all about the inner workings of our Great Stores now that I've had a peep behind the scenes. "The Far Side of the Counter" – how's that for a title?'

So I only hope that no libel actions are pending, though I doubt if she can do much damage, with the best intentions in the world. If she'd really been behind the scenes, of course, she'd have had a very much better story for her Federated Women. Mine, for instance. I've just had another spectacular rise.

My scheme for improving the Library began it. I sent in a very discreet and modest memorandum, no names, of course, but quite disruptive. It was a really concise, dry-as-dust report for the Minor Prophet; all headings and numbers and cause and effect. Together with a sketch map of desks and shelves, and facts about waste of space and undusted corners and classification of subscribers. I used my imagination and sent the thing in, very proud and nervous.

Authority approved. The scheme is to be carried out almost to the last detail, but it has been considered wise to inaugurate the reforms as from headquarters, and safer for me to be out of the Library altogether while they're in progress.

It was partly that and partly because Miss Ward's Assistant Staff Supervisor has got engaged and downed tools on the strength of it that I've been moved up again. What I owe to appendicitis and holy matrimony, Basil! I've got the engaged one's job.

Isn't it grand? It means getting back to the sort of organising work that I really enjoy. Also, one comes less into physical contact with books and ink and labels and typewriters, which is so fortunate, considering how much I'm at the mercy of the malice of the inanimate.

Of course, the immediate result of the change hasn't been imposing, so far. I've been running round after Miss Ward, carrying her pencil on her tours of inspection, making notes on the state of staff lavatories, the number of assistants absent and why, ringing up obscure departments to send people to show tongues to Sister Smith, running a finger along window-sills to demonstrate to cleaners where they've become weary in well doing, and chivvying typists out of the cloakrooms. 'Training me,' Miss Ward calls it. And it's been most illuminating. I feel that I'm beginning to have an idea of the *fabric* of the business: it's thrilling because everything's woven into it; pots and pans and silks and carpets and wood and brass and sales books and typewriters and people's lives. I

'CHIVVYING TYPISTS OUT OF CLOAK-ROOMS'

don't suppose I shall ever write: 'Dear sir, – Will you send me a cake of soap to the above address and charge my account. Yours faithfully ...' quite unthinkingly again. I shall always see the wheels that I inspected this morning grip my letter and hurry it away.

I went with Miss Ward to the Mail Order Department (the Central Mail Orders, of course, not the Book Floor's own very minor corner run by Mr Simpson and company.) The central Mail Order Department is housed on the other side of Manifold Lane, in a hygienic, red brick building, mostly windows. A covered way runs above the garages across to the main block, and trolleys thunder along it from nine to six. We walked gingerly among them, and a child (Miss Ward called her a Query Clerk) swung open doors for us.

'Mail Orders,' said Miss Ward, with a casual flip of a finger towards the immense, grey room.

'All of it?' (That single department runs across the thickness of two buildings, back to back, from Manifold Lane to Severn Street.)

'We deal with seven thousand letters a day in the course of ordinary routine,' said Miss Ward. 'And twelve thousand in a rush season. Sales, you know, and Christmas.' I believed her. That room looked like the photographs of the Irish Sweep on Mixing Day. There was a sort of horse trough running down one side of it and divided into a dozen alphabetically labelled compartments. Six girls shovelled letters into the compartments, six more snatched them out, pounded them with rubber stamps, shot them into trays marked SOFT FURNISHINGS; PIECE GOODS; TURNERY; JUVENILE; GOWNS; FURNISHING FABRICS ... and so on. Boys with satchels came round and grabbed them out to take them to the right place in the main store.

The last tray was marked TO BE DISSECTED: a young man collected the letters in it and took them to a long table. Here four other harassed-looking young men were dealing with the letters of people who had been thoughtless enough to order silk stockings and pillow slips and tinned peaches and writing paper on the same letter. The men flapped catalogues and wrote the orders down on forms with the name of the department printed enormously at the top and carbons underneath. Everybody's lightest wish is recorded there, world without end, and the dissected, original letter goes to be filed, in a maze of rubber stamps. It's humbling to watch it all: if it weren't for the fallible human factor, it'd be nearly perfect as a system.

Miss Ward insisted on telling me all about it when I just wanted to stand and soak in all its exciting complexity instead. Then a very small man with the inevitable bowler came up and distracted her attention so that I could gape undisturbed. He sounded plaintive.

'I can't do it,' he said. 'Not without I have another clerk. Them four' – he jerked a thumb at the toiling dissectors with their catalogues – 'just can't keep up with the orders. They're two hundred behind as it is, aren't you, Thomas?'

'One hundred and eighty,' said Thomas, licking his fingers and whirling from the Fashion Shoes to the Perambulators.

'It's this Character from your Handwriting what does it,' said the man in the bowler. He waved a double sheet of dark-blue, crested paper splattered with hieroglyphics at us. 'Here's an order as long as your arm from yours faithfully Gawd-knows-wot.'

'Don't they ever type?' asked Miss Ward.

'Do they not! With their feet by the look of it. No, the only hope for most people'd be block caps. And now, miss, wot about that clerk you promised me?'

'Well, will you have a man or a girl?' said Miss Ward, taking out her note-book. 'I can get you a couple of nice girls by this afternoon.'

The small man's voice rose to a squeak. 'No, Miss Ward, I

will not have a gel. I've told you before how it is. I can't do with gels. Not on this job. They talk too much. Sifting's about their mark. Can't do much harm without bein' noticed by somebody, even if it's only them Jimmys.' And he jerked his bowler at the scuttling boys.

Miss Ward said she'd see to it, quite meekly, I thought, and I made a note in my book. We went on to the next section. This room was lined with steel bins belching parcels.

'The Assembling Room,' said Miss Ward.

All the bits of dissected orders come here to join up, and are packed in boxes and put on a moving band that takes them on to the Packing Room, which is a sort of primeval chaos of brown paper, shavings, straw and string. It's staffed by very large men in shirt sleeves who make up packages, slap labels on their sides and heave them on to a sort of moving staircase which empties them into the goods lift.

After that we went to some of the Store Rooms, where part of the stock is kept before it reaches departmental shelves. Things like gowns and cosmetics and lingerie live in the main building, but all the bulky items, like garden rollers and crates of cheap and nasty china to be found in the humbler seaside lodgings and impoverished 'quaint' tea-rooms are stored on the far side of Manifold Lane.

One of the biggest and hottest of shirt-sleeved men came up to us with his bowler pushed well back and a red rim bitten into his forehead. He positively scolded Miss Ward, and I prepared for thunderbolts which somehow didn't come.

'Now, look 'ere, miss,' he said. 'Wot about them gels you promised me? Day before yesterday it wos that I spoke, and I asks you now, w'ere are they? Wot I wants to know is can I count on you for six gels this afternoon or can I not? Because

'WOT ABOUT THEM GELS?'

if not how's the best line of bedroom china we've bought this year to be unpacked? I've got to 'ave 'ands. I mean, I put it to *you*, can you expect a miracle to get the paper off them lovely ewers and …'

'I quite see,' said Miss Ward. 'And I'll send you all the help you want. I've got a string from the Labour Exchange outside my door this minute.'

'Gels!' said the large, hot man to himself as we went away. 'Try the patience more'n a cats' concert. You can always take your boots to a cat …'

After that we went back across the covered way among the trolleys and errand boys. 'We'd better have a look at what the Labour Exchange has brought,' Miss Ward said. Rather as if she were going to pinch arms in the slave market, I thought, remembering that same Labour Exchange and my feelings there.

'Have you ever done any interviewing?'

I said, 'Yes.' And Miss Ward said, 'Oh.' And we walked on.

But as we were going up to her room in the Lift, she said: 'Well, I think you might help me by weeding out some of the obviously hopeless ones. You can have the room next to mine and send away anybody who looks unfit or mentally deficient.'

Could one be given a more dreary job? But I could hardly refuse. So I gathered paper and a pen and my most official expression, and went into the room next to Miss Ward's. Then I told the first in the queue to go to Miss Ward and the next to come to me. The rest of that morning is a story in itself, and too long to add to this letter. Because if I miscalculate and it's too heavy, Mrs MacQueen is quite fit to return it to the postman before you have time to appear grandly and say that to a man of your means a penny is neither here nor there. Rather than risk that I'll tell you about the interviewing next time.

H

EVERYMAN'S STORES

OXFORD STREET

W1

'Our business is your pleasure.'

November 22st
Saturday morning

BASIL DEAR

This is an extra letter, wrongfully written in the firm's time and on the firm's best notepaper. I've never been grand enough to use either for letters before. But now I'm writing in my own office, at my own desk. If, that's to say, one can so glorify the six-foot space between two frosted glass partitions, a window and a door. Probably it used to be a stationery store, for brown paper parcels fill the shelves along one wall and people rush up now and then to ask if they may take one away. But the half-glass door has been newly painted, and to sit and spell out ASSISTANT STAFF SUPERVISOR backwards is worth any number of boxes of envelopes and quires of typing paper.

I still have to poke out occasional letters on the typewriter myself, of course. Which is not so grand. I cope with Miss Ward's more compromising memoranda, all about the greater members of the firm, which is often rather terrifying. I look at buyers like Mrs Banbury, and wonder if she can really be going to have her teeth out at Easter and what she'd think if she knew that I knew about it. People have such a complex about teeth. If they're having an appendix out or a toe off they talk to you about it, willy nilly, for months. But teeth are only extracted in secret. I suppose it's these advertisements for disinfectants that 'do the work while you sleep', and the thought that any burglar would have you entirely at his mercy till you found the tumbler.

Then I still have to carry Miss Ward's pencil and make notes for her when she tours the departments. But she also expects me to do a certain amount of what she calls 'weeding' among the applicants from the Labour Exchanges, and that means that I have to look over the ten most unlikely creatures, and try to think of ten ways of telling them that they haven't a chance.

It doesn't usually surprise them. Some are so obviously unfitted for any but the brighter professions.

Some are straight from school, drearily submerged in mother's cast-off coat and almost any sort of hat: and some are just those aimlessly stubborn people who resent any effort to employ them. When they've demanded employment and been refused the matter ends. I had one of them this morning: she seemed rather more hopeful than most. So I said that we might be able to do something for her if she were less untidy.

She said: 'Quite all right, thank you, miss. I'm on the Dole. Sign my card, please.'

But one child looked so wretched when I said no that I took it back, and let her go on to see Miss Ward. But Miss Ward just said: 'My dear Miss Fane, why on earth did you bother me with her? Didn't you see her *feet*?' So then I stayed and listened to Miss Ward interviewing her batch of applicants. No mere customer realises the elements of a successful Lift Girl even after years of watching the contemptuous young women in blue leather breeches and silver piped Eton jackets who run ours. But Miss Ward has a way of unerringly selecting Lift Girls in embryo from the rows of shiny-hatted, brass-buttoned young women who present themselves. She has flair: she just knows that for some reason not apparent to the rest of humanity one young woman has the elements of a successful Lift Girl or a Query Clerk or an assistant for the Gramophones or Wireless or Lingerie or Perfumes or the makings of a waitress or a Rest Room attendant, and the twin next her hasn't. So useful. I blunder along by taking thought, but the results haven't been nearly as good so far.

Now and then, when I've dismissed one queue and my next job isn't too imperative, things are quiet in my office, and I can look out of the window which is the best thing in it – apart from its being new and mine. The window looks over Manifold Lane and the garages and the Stock-and-Store Rooms that belong to us and all the small shops on the far side of the Lane which don't.

There's a barber's saloon and a pub and a grocer's and an antique shop crammed with oddities; plush chairs and bronze statuettes and palm pots and milking stools and witch bowls and old pictures and muskets and finger-bowls and china figures and a pale ivory crucifix and candlesticks and chessmen. And there's a mirror that's tilted up this morning to reflect an oval of clear sky with puffs of cloud.

When I walk down the Lane at lunch time I always see an old man sitting in a back room reading his paper among all the frowsty bits of things and some perfectly lovely pewter. He never seems to sell anything, or to mind.

Three or four barrel organs are always upended outside the pub, and sometimes a flower seller leaves his tray of out-of-season snowdrops tied up with ivy leaves outside too. Which seems rash. But nobody notices them.

And I'd no idea till I got my office how many people earn a living by singing 'Annie Laurie'. They walk up and down the Lane between the barrel organs and sing outside the pub till they've got enough pennies to go inside it. Then someone comes out to claim his barrel organ and goes off down the Lane with it. Presently a cheerful, tinny tune gets the better of the gearchanging outside the garages. I suppose barrel organs will mean Manifold Lane to me for the rest of my life.

Later

I was interrupted then by the Head Post Girl, who's lean and thirty-five, but will be a girl, ex-officio, till she's superannuated. She tramped into my office and presented a sniffling junior clerk more or less by the ear. Presumably she had told the child what she thought of her on the stairs. At any rate, she had no breath left when she arrived, and could only thump a letter and an envelope zig-zagged with post-marks in front of me and point at her victim. Then she stood there, purpling, while the poor little clerk quivered and squeaked.

I picked up the letter. It was one of our more effusive ones and the customer had sent it back, enclosing our envelope, which she had covered with the sort of hand-writing typical of one's moneyed aunts. Part of it was a further order, but the last sentence said:

'I think it only *kind* to tell your clerk that it costs 2½d to send letters abroad.'

Of course I was paralysed. It struck me as comic, but rather less than kind. There was a pause. 'After six weeks on the post,' said the Post Girl. And waited expectantly. I was blank. Miss Ward would have seized the opportunity for a talk on the importance and inter-dependence of detail and discipline and duty. But I only wished that they'd dealt with the crime in the Post and Despatch. Finally, I said that if the Post Girl weren't there to supervise, the other clerks would be sending out letters without any stamps at all. That must have struck home, for she went. And left me with the criminal, longing to laugh. Finally, I pulled myself together and asked her if she'd anything to say. I believe that's always done by Inquisitors, from one's first nurse to the hanging judge. But she just burrowed in the pocket of her overall and bleated: 'I'll never be able to stamp another letter right, I know I won't.' Which seemed so likely that I looked up her dossier and the Staff List, and turned her into an errand girl on the spot, changing a very tough errand girl, who'd done well at school, into a post clerk. I only hope that Miss Ward won't go through her records till it's past history, and I can say: 'Oh, don't you remember making that alteration?' with some hope of carrying conviction.

By the way, did I tell you that I was going to change my rooms again? That flat has been at the back of my mind ever since I got my first extra pay. And now I've found it – two rooms and a kit-bath where you fry your bacon in one corner and turn on your bath in the other and iron things on the bath lid. Most compact and not necessarily sordid. The present tenants haven't moved out yet, which suits me, as I shall move in over the New Year, much as I'd like to be settled in before Christmas. But with the rush beginning next month, and an hour's overtime every night up to Christmas Eve, I doubt if anything like a move would be humanly possible.

I hope you'll like the flat: it's at the top of one of the houses in Christchurch Street, Chelsea. The river's only half a street away, so that I'll hear the water slapping at the Embankment on quiet nights and the steamers always. Unfurnished, of course, but better people than I have set up house with a bed and a packing-case. Rent thirty shillings a week. Gas fires, unfortunately, but the meter's decently hidden in the cupboard and, anyway, I'll rip one out of the sitting-room. I must have one coal fire.

What do you think about Christmas? Will you be as busy as you were last year? Or is it impossible to tell? Would you like to come to us over the week-end? I must see something of the family and as much as I can of you and that might be a way out of the difficulty. But I suppose if you have to be at Christopher's a lot, Mrs MacQueen's is more convenient, being on the doorstep.

Do just what you think. But come if you can.

H

EVERYMAN'S STORES

For use in inter-departmental correspondence only

From M E Ward *To* Miss Fane
November 23rd, 1931

Subject Seating accommodation for Clerical Staff (Book Floor)

Memo

It has been brought to my notice that a number of chairs in use by the Clerical Staff are of an inconvenient size and that some clerks are in the habit of bringing cushions to sit on.

Please report on the necessity for these.

M E WARD

BT/MEW

EVERYMAN'S STORES

For use in inter-departmental correspondence only

From H Fane   *To* Miss Ward
                              November 23rd, 1931

Subject What our typists sit on

Memo

I have to report that no chairs in the Clerical Department, Book Floor, seem to be the right height, size or shape for people who type. The following expedients are in use:

Miss Dowland sits on a pink cushion provided by herself.

Miss Hopper sits on a jersey and Roget's Thesaurus. Her chair is intrinsically high enough, and she does not type much, but she says that the seat is cold and therefore injurious to her health.

Miss Watts sits on *Aristotle*.

Miss Lamb sits on Gibbon's *Decline and Fall*, Vol 3.

Mr Millett sits on a packing-case.

Mr Simpson sits on his coat.

There is a good case for cushions, except perhaps for Mr Simpson who should not be encouraged to sit, and Mr Millett, who hardly ever does, and prefers a packing-case, anyway.

23 BURFORD STREET
WC1

November 26th

MY DEAR BASIL,

I'm writing most uncomfortably, with my hair hanging over my face in wet strands and dripping on to my paper. I've been swimming. In the depths of winter. Definitely heroic, don't you think? I admit that the idea wasn't mine: actually I was more or less shamed into it by Mary Meldon. We had been discussing the difficulty of playing games in London over one of our rapid lunches, and I was mourning the lost grand days when I'd been rather good at hockey, and giving the impression (without actual boasting) that I hadn't been bad at anything athletic. But what with the hour it took to get to any club ground and the other hour it took to get back, and the time wasted over tea and team sociabilities, I couldn't bear to think of giving a whole half-Saturday to getting exercise. I said it was incredibly unfortunate, but by the end of the winter I should look like one of those long, white, unhealthy bits of grass that survive under planks.

Mary Meldon said: 'My dear, that's quite true.' (Which I thought unkind.) 'And what you ought to do is to swim. It only takes half an hour, after work, and you feel you could push a street down when you come out.'

I said, 'Really?' And Mary said, *'Really!'* in the tone that people use when they mean to make you do something for your good, from trying a new face cream to buying a house. I struggled feebly, but I knew it was all settled. We arranged to meet at the Oxford Street end of Manifold Lane, at six o'clock on Thursday. Mary said she would take me to her favourite baths. Quite new, she told me. And warm.

That sounded reasonable, but this evening it rained and the cold pounced round the corner at me as soon as I came out of the Staff Entrance. I blundered along Manifold Lane, praying that she wouldn't be there, or wouldn't see me or something, so that I could climb into a bus and be carried safely home. But:

'*Here* you are, darling. Marvellous!' said Mary. 'Just the night for a swim. The colder it is outside the better one feels afterwards.' (Which struck me as just nonsense.) 'We'll take a penny bus – people won't believe it, of course, but one does. Glad *you've* got some sense.'

Obviously there was to be no escape.

'People are just *sheep*,' said Mary. 'They get an idea that because it's a cold day it's going to be cold in the water. All rubbish. Here's our stop.'

We climbed out into the east wind again. By the time we'd reached the baths I'd drafted the telegrams which would bring you and the family to my bedside before pleurisy carried me off.

'Tickets ninepence to-night,' said Mary. 'Mixed. You get two towels.'

I surrendered my ninepence and took my two hard, dish-cloth-like bits of towel feeling most unwilling to be butchered just to provide Mary with her holiday. But it seemed useless to protest so we went through swing doors into a sort of wet Bedlam. The bath was really enormous, new and white marblish, with a great ruffled oblong of startlingly blue water under the arc lights in a remote domed roof. 'The disinfectant makes it that colour,' said Mary unnecessarily, as I was enjoying it.

There were ranks of seats mounting to the dressing cubicles, which were indiscreet little hutches with wooden doors as far up as your waist and curtains after that.

As we climbed up the nearest stair I had that uncomfortable feeling that something was wrong somewhere, but I couldn't think what it was till an attendant chased after me to say that we were forcing our way into the GENTS ONLY section. I was covered by confusion but Mary said they ought to have a placard up on Mixed Nights. Could we be expected to know by instinct? And, anyway, wasn't it just like men to charge you an extra penny, because they'd be there too!

I took as long as I dared to undress, but finally I had to crawl out and Mary shamed me into jumping in with eyes and mouth screwed shut because of that disinfectant. But she pranced on to the spring-board, and did an irrelevant handspring into the water. Once in, it really was rather marvellous. I began to believe all the things that Mary said about winter swimming. Movement through that blue, warmed water is such a queer, clean pleasure. I decided to take real exercise, and started swimming lengths. But I'd calculated without the other athletes and kept being beset by the young women who hurled themselves off the side, approximately parallel with the water, and raised frightful fountains just in front of me.

Nearer the shallow end there were groups of non-swimmers, or chin-held performers, who stood about waist-deep, talking passionately. I just kicked those obstacles in the stomach and swam on. But the deep end, on the return journeys, was very terrifying. Dozens of Greekish young men were propped up against the high diving boards, looking like statuary, except that every now and then one of them would come to life and wander up the ladder to the very highest board. He'd stand a bit there and push back a wet forelock and pummel his muscles while I frogged despairingly out of the way, miles below. Eventually he'd launch himself off with a couple of somersaults or a sideways twist or a jackknife touch-toes-and-out movement. This happened nearly all the time. Sometimes they shouted 'Hi!' and sometimes not.

It was all very dangerous.

I did four lengths, quite humbly, between the splashes, and Mary kept up the credit of the party by taking turns with the young men for the spring-boards, and allowed people to show her new dives and was thoroughly athletic.

Afterwards we went and had an enormous, crazy meal of tea and bacon and eggs and bread and butter and honey and plum cake at a small restaurant which makes rather a good thing out of dripping, ravenous people from the baths. I told Mary at least half a dozen times that life was worth living, and I meant to swim every Thursday evening for the rest of the winter. And she was heroically enthusiastic every time.

But now my hair's dry I shall have to go to bed. All my muscles are feeling stretched and warm, and I'm sleepy beyond possible resistance. It's lovely to feel as well as this. Do you suppose that fish race about rivers and jump out of sheer glorification, or is it the dreary, natural history of catching flies after all?

Now – SLEEP … darling.

HILARY

EVERYMAN'S STORES

OXFORD STREET

WI

'Our business is your pleasure.'

November 27th

BASIL MY DEAR,

I'm bothered. Badly. I've let myself in for something more than I can cope with on my own. And till I remembered you and Christopher's, I was scared.

Mildred Lamb came to see me this morning. I think I've written about her; that rather nice child from the Book Floor Clerical. She said she wouldn't have dared speak to Miss Ward or to Sister. But I was different. She was in trouble: wanted advice. Of course I've met this Victorian complication before, but it was startling to find that it could obtrude itself in these sophisticated surroundings. Surely typists don't have babies; even on the films? Miss Lamb isn't a likely victim either: she's a semi-educated, competent, but badly frightened young woman with no family and a landlady out at Cricklewood with 'her own living to earn'. It's the sort of crisis in which the shillings in the Superannuation Fund won't help much. Neither will Authority. Authority might shame the two into marrying each other, but Mildred is honest enough to admit that she doesn't want to. She's perfectly willing to accept the consequences if somebody will tell her what to do. And I think that sort of attitude always appeals, don't you? All convictions apart, I mean.

So I told her rashly that I'd see to it, without an idea in

my head except that the situation had to be coped with, as reasonably as possible. This afternoon I thought of you.

She'll leave, of course. But if you could take her into Christopher's later on, I gather that an obscure Scots aunt might help her afterwards. Then her savings would probably last till she got another job, perhaps in Edinburgh.

I told her, futilely, not to worry. But you'll let me know what you think you'll be able to arrange for her quite soon, won't you? I'm going to post this on my way home, so I won't write more. This isn't a letter, just an SOS.

With my love,

HILARY

EVERYMAN'S STORES

For use in inter-departmental correspondence only

From M G Grant   *To* Miss Fane
                                    December 2nd, 1931

Subject Miss Lamb, C. 284. Book Floor

Memo. CONFIDENTIAL

In accordance with this morning's request I will arrange for Miss Lamb to draw out the total amount of her Superannuation payments at the end of March. She may then take a month's holiday on full pay prior to her resignation for reasons of health. I will then make a recommendation to a doctor of my acquaintance.

In your place, I should advise her to try to obtain work in Scotland when she wishes to take another post. If she is not successful, she may apply to me.

M G G

NS/MGG

23 **BURFORD STREET**

December 2nd

DEAR BASIL,

I disagree with you entirely. But your letter leaves no more to be said, does it? Except that your attitude to 'such sentimentality gone mad' is fortunately not universal, and I have been successful in making other arrangements.

HILARY

EVERYMAN'S STORES

OXFORD STREET

W1

'Our business is your pleasure.'

December 10th

DEAREST MUMMY AND DADDY,

I'm writing at once to make sure of the country post. I've just been arranging my holiday. Most people get from Thursday, after work, to Monday morning. But what with one thing and what with another and being Scots and looking tired I've got till Wednesday! Nobody who hasn't worked in Oxford Street knows what an Immense Concession those two days are. If it hadn't been for Sister Smith weighing me and shaking her head I doubt if Miss Ward could have put through the recommendation. But Sister Smith said, most reasonably, that it'd be worth the firm's while for the work I'd do afterwards. And Miss Ward's so surprised and pleased at my usefulness that she agreed at once.

Tell Basil when you see him, so that he can arrange to be free. Letters are impossible just now.

In a fortnight I'll report in person.

So much love,

HILARY

BURFORD BASEMENT

December 16th

MY DEAR,

I'm sorry not to have written to you for the last fortnight, but as you only wrote once yourself I don't feel really guilty. And what Aunt Bertha calls the Far Side of the Counter is not a leisured place during the Christmas season.

Miss Ward says she's run off her feet, so I've been promoted from carrying her pencil and making her notes and weeding out the unsuitable applicants to engaging extra staff on my own. Which is much more cheerful. It's so much easier to say:

'Yes. Report for work to-morrow. Health and Unemployment cards, of course,' than the dreary:

'I'm afraid ...'

And then, in my official capacity I have to take the pulse of at least a dozen departments daily, and decide whether their buyers are really overdriven and under-staffed as well as proclaiming to heaven that life is intolerable and their one desire a decently quiet grave. I settle disputes, administer sal volatile and good advice, placate and guide any customers I may meet clamouring for mechanical toys among the ironmongery. And so few people have the remotest capacity for grasping directions. Tell a couple of harassed aunts that the Crackers and Caps are 'Straight through, second on the left' and they set off, go through two archways, turn to the right and arrive, flustered and unbelieving, among the Perfumes and Bath Salts.

And nobody reads notices. Ours are so blatant, too. Enormous red and white placards sprayed with holly hang just high enough to miss people's heads, but nobody ever lifts a nose the necessary two inches. We might as well not have printed things like:

PRESENTS FOR HIM	FIRST TO THE LEFT
PRESENTS FOR HER	SECOND ON THE RIGHT
BOOKS FOR BAD BROTHERS	FIFTH FLOOR UP
BARGAINS DOWNSTAIRS	

They always ask: they always choose an assistant who is audibly adding: and they leave snowdrifts of nameless lists among the Gents' Haberdashery or the Handbags and Umbrellas. Such anxious, calculating things they are, with rows of names and ticks and prices and question marks.

Silk stockings for Beryl, say 5/11?

Bath salts for Aunt Mary (if cheque)

Mrs Jameson. Calendar. (Or shilling card?)

The assistants gather them up philosophically and send them to Inquiries in sheaves with a 'Wait till called for' notice on them. And on the 27th of December, I understand, they are summarily destroyed.

The Temporary Staff, heaven help them, all develop an appalling tendency to add on their fingers in a crisis. (Just like me.) I suggest fiercely that if they must use their fingers they might have the grace to barricade themselves behind a showcase. Some customers *mind* so. Of course some laugh, and this morning I heard one humane woman in the Provisions say to a terrified Temporary: 'Look here, you seem to hate arithmetic as much as I do. If we did that sum together we might manage, don't you think?' Salt of the earth!

But can you wonder at things like manual arithmetic and those occasional flares of temper when you remember how exhausted everyone is? I've kept Christmas with the best but I've never *provided* it before. I hadn't an idea what December could be like for the people who did. I looked down from the third floor gallery this morning in half a second's lull: the ground floor was solid with desperate-looking people – screwing heads and jutting elbows and flapping lists on one side of the counters, and a rattish scurry of assistants on the other.

And the evenings are pandemonium. That's the worst of all this rivalry in illuminated, jack-in-the-box window-dressing. Such crowds come to watch our life-sized Father Christmas sledging across electrically moon-lit roofs to drop presents down real chimneys. What's the use of exhorting the suburbs to shop early when the fun doesn't begin till after dark? And it certainly helps to fill the basements with bargain hunters. Most of our girls don't get home before ten o'clock at night during the weeks before Christmas. And no number of overtime shillings make up for the strain of that sort of a day.

Well, there it is. I expect the family's told you that my particular holiday is to be specially extended till Wednesday morning. I shall travel north by night on Thursday and come south by night on Tuesday. That'll give us five complete days together, which will be much better really, than the snippets of evenings and the short week-ends we'd have had if you'd been able to come up to London when I wanted you to. (That's not to mean, of course, that I despise any such evenings or week-ends that may be possible in the future. It's just present vainglory.)

Five days at home! When I think of it the toes curl inside my shoes with excitement. I love night journeys. I know they're either stuffy or arctic: I don't sleep and the other women snore: I always arrive looking filthy and hag looking. But it's so marvellous to get into my sleeper (3rd class) at Euston and out of it in Edinburgh. I wouldn't miss a single uncomfortable, anticipatory minute. I like watching everything before we start. The platform's mounded with H M Mails and pillows, and people's queer luggage. There's a good minute when the train begins to rock across the points … Oh, *fun*, Basil.

All my love,

HILARY

UNIVERSITY CLOSE
EDINBURGH

December 28th, 1931

I'm sorry I didn't come to the station, my dear. I admit that I was rather sore. Can you wonder, on the whole? I've come north, for the first week-end since September to find that you've arranged to rush to London on Sunday night for a conference and banquet. Nothing dragged you there during the four months I've been south, but you leave me here at a moment's notice and pay London a twenty-four hours' visit because of an invitation which had been lying forgotten in some pigeon-hole for the last six weeks, and found by accident two days ago.

You must know how proud I am when you're asked to grand functions of that kind. And I'd hate to feel that I kept you from them. But if I'd *known* – if you'd had the sense to ask me what my plans were when that invitation came I'd have arranged to take the extra day before Christmas instead of after it.

I can hardly alter my arrangements now. After all, I haven't seen the Family for four months either, and when they've killed so many fatted calves for my homecoming I can't leave them to eat the carcases alone. So I'll travel down on Tuesday night as I told you.

H

Train

December 29th

DEAREST MUMMY AND DADDY,

Another of those train-written letters! I apologise. Still, you've brought this one on yourselves. But for your representations I'd be travelling south to-night, and harmlessly asleep. This is a criminal way of spending a whole day of my specially stretched-out Christmas leave. Nothing but your lurid descriptions of my exhausted state and certain blunders after a night in the train would have persuaded me to allow such an anti-climax. Probably one day isn't a tragic sacrifice, either, but this journey's a gruesome end to any holiday, you'll admit.

We're crashing through the Midlands now, past slag-heaps and pools scummed with empty tins and cigarette cartons and twisted, hopeless bits of iron and old boots. Rows of drearily identical little houses have their washing flapping among the smuts. If I were going north instead of south, I'd be noticing the way the sunset circles the carriage as the train swings round, and the gas flares tossed about high in the air outside factories, and the furnace-red inside them. But you know how I hate things ending. Even holidays.

It's been a grand week-end: you've both been so lovely to me. And the last two days have been more of a rest than they could have been if Basil hadn't had to go south so unexpectedly.

After three months in digs it's been so marvellous to be able to go up and downstairs and along the passages of a house that wasn't divided up among a dozen irrelevant lives. So nice to smell dog and books again, too, instead of kippers and people's washing. There's something about home meals, apart from knowing that nobody'll come up to you with a bill afterwards. (Though that's a comfort too.) I hate eating in restaurants – one reason why I'm looking forward to having my flat. I take possession on the first of January. Did I tell you? Lovely, but think of the flitting!

Does anybody collect junk as infallibly and chronically as our family? Not with any particular end in view, I mean, like jumble sales or things Coming in Useful. Just cheerful magpieness. I came into Burford Street three months ago with one big suitcase and one little one, but I don't see how I can possibly get out of it without a pantechnicon.

I hadn't even the sense to annex an extra trunk this morning, from the glory-hole under the stairs. I shall importune the local grocer for packing-cases, so on and after the first of the year write to me in Chelsea. I'll be there – in the intervals of carting possessions across London.

With very much love,

HILARY

CHELSEA

January 2nd, 1932

MY DEAR BASIL,

Am I to take your letter as an ultimatum? I understand that you accuse me of spending four months in a picnic existence of which you tried to show your disapproval from the first, and therefore you resent my calling you inconsiderate. Evidently you were merely applying my own methods when you left Scotland last Sunday.

You also consider that I try to use your professional prestige for my own convenience (that's Mildred Lamb, I suppose). Also that I am sentimental, illogical and unbalanced.

I'm repeating what you wrote, not because I want to be dramatic or anything, but only to make sure that you both wrote and meant those things – of me.

I'd like to know, please.

HILARY

BUSINESS AS USUAL   PART II – WINTER

From the records of H M Post Office

January 7th, 1932

Regn. No. 3126

Certificate of posting of a registered Postal Packet.

A postal packet addressed as under, upon which a fee of threepence has been paid, in addition to the postage of .... (for parcels only) has been registered and posted here this day:—

Date Stamp.

BASIL RAINFORD, ESQ., | *7th Ja.*
EDINBURGH | *32*

Accepting Officer's Signature...A.P.S.

Part III – Spring

PART III – SPRING

2A CHRISTCHURCH STREET
CHELSEA

January 22nd

DEAREST FAMILY,

I don't know whether you have any chairs that you're not actually sitting on, but if you have I'd welcome them. Somehow, one doesn't realise how many things there ought to be in a room till one takes possession of three entirely empty ones, and goes echoing about with pots of distemper for a week. There was a vast pile of luggage when I loaded up at Burford Street; what happened to it on the journey I can't imagine.

So I've been spending all my lunch hours in or about Woolworth's. It's a mercy that they send orders over six shillings, as I could hardly go back to Everyman's hung round with ironmongery. The kitchen's filling up nicely, and I've got a bed with the sheets and blankets I brought south, and the three big packing-cases the grocer gave me. They make lovely tables, but rather unsympathetic chairs. And there are all my college things – a trifle æsthetic and skimpy. Still, they include four bowls for bulbs and several cushions. So I was surprised and hurt when my new charlady asked for a day's money in advance before she took her hat off.

I said that I was furnishing by degrees, and she said so she supposed, but had I seen the lovely sofas they gave you on the Hire Purchase System? She couldn't understand, apparently, how any creature could prefer packing-cases to leatherette and fumed oak.

After that she revolved on her axis and demanded dusters. And mops. And leathers. And scrubbing soap. All the things I'd forgotten to get at Woolworths. So I sent her out to get them on the King's Road. She came back before I'd finished my breakfast and laid them out in front of me happily, like a good retriever. I left for work feeling that I'd acquired a Household. Weighed down, you know, but proud.

I'm having Mrs Bland for two hours every morning and three evenings a week. So, with three really filling suppers a week I can afford to dabble in cookery between whiles. That row of Woolworth pans demands experiment.

I've a lot to do, you see, quite without manufacturing any of those dreary occupations which must be so much worse, on the whole, than doing nothing. And I did appreciate what you said in your letter about Basil. I knew you'd take my word for it that our engagement had to end, but I hadn't counted on such unqualified support. It's most sustaining.

Lots of love,

HILARY

EVERYMAN'S STORES

For use in inter-departmental correspondence only

From M E Ward *To* Mr Grant
February 2nd, 1932

Subject Assistant Staff Supervisor, Miss Fane

Memo

In reply to your inquiry of yesterday's date I am finding Miss Fane a capable assistant.

I am pleased to be able to say she did very well during the Christmas rush, when I was compelled to leave more responsible work in her hands than I would otherwise have done.

She is thoroughly reliable, pleasant and tactful in her dealings with the staff. Perhaps she is inclined to allow her sense of humour to run away with her, but time and experience will no doubt remedy this.

I am quite in agreement with you in thinking that it would be wise to confirm her appointment, and that her salary should be increased by a further 10/- per week.

M E WARD
Staff Supervisor

BT/MBW

BUSINESS AS USUAL

EVERYMAN'S STORES

For use in inter-departmental correspondence only

From M G Grant

To Miss Fane
February 3rd, 1932

Subject Your appointment as Asst. Staff Supervisor

Memo

You will have heard from Miss Ward that your appointment has been confirmed, and I am glad to be able to tell you that her report on your work is very satisfactory.

Now that the Christmas rush is over, it will be possible to complete the reorganisation of the Library and Rational Reading Services at present under consideration. I shall require you to supervise this work in person, and should therefore like to discuss the various aspects of it with you.

I expect to be free about 3.30 this afternoon, but perhaps you would ring up my office before you come, in case I should have been delayed.

M G GRANT

SN/MGG

I have been given to understand that Time and Experience arc expected to modify your sense of humour, but cannot see that such modification would serve any useful purpose.

M G G

PART III – SPRING

EVERYMAN'S STORES

For use in inter-departmental correspondence only

From H Fane *To* Mr Grant
February 4th, 1932

Subject Library: Book Floor

Memo (Unofficial)

With reference to our conversation yesterday, I have spent several hours in investigations connected with the Library, and believe your theory of a passive boycott to be well founded.

The new system is now in working order, but the difficulty is that no one wants to work it.

Miss Sparling can't be induced to offer an opinion, except that she has always done her best. Miss Hopper says it's always the way, she's often thought herself that things could be improved, but when you came to alter them you see that there's a very good reason for leaving them the way they were. Miss Landry, of whom I had hopes, has obviously been terrorised into hostility towards reforms which look like meaning more work.

If I'm to cope with this situation I must have more authority. Miss Sparling, round whom the hostility centres, must see that I can, if necessary, import as many clerks as I need, and that, therefore, she ceases to be indispensable. As a friend of mine says, there's nothing like an unimpeded view of the gutter for bringing people round.

H F

EVERYMAN'S STORES

For use in inter-departmental correspondence only

From M G Grant *To* Miss Ward

February 5th, 1932

Subject Reorganisation of the Library

Memo

Miss Fane has my authority – to be exercised with your knowledge and consent – personally to choose and to appoint as many new Library clerks as she may find necessary. She may also give orders to the firm's carpenters and other workmen for the installation of new desks, shelves and placards which may be required for the reorganisation of the Library which she has undertaken.

She will, I know, be grateful for any advice which may appear to you necessary, but I should prefer the matter to be undertaken by her alone, provided that she does not allow zeal to outrun discretion.

M G GRANT

SN/MGG

2A CHRISTCHURCH STREET
CHELSEA

February 10th

MY DEAR AUNT BERTHA,

To think that I never suspected why you were asking me all those questions over lunch last Sunday – apart, I mean, from housewifely fellow-feeling about the size and number of my windows and the shape of my rooms!

Until to-night! Even then, when I came home and found that one of our own blue vans had emptied itself up those uncertainly railed stairs, I just thought that somebody connected with Post and Despatch would probably get the sack for leaving a lordly order at the wrong house. But the labels were quite explicit about my name and address. And every bale had a pleasant green tag which said NO BILL — THIS IS A PRESENT.

I dragged them all inside my sitting-room and chewed at sacking and string with a pair of nail-scissors, and stamped about on brown paper in quite tremendous excitement.

Of course gratitude is a poor, orphanish sort of word to express my sensations when I'd unpacked that carpet, the two arm-chairs, the four cushions and two pairs of curtains! A few yards of material or some old loose-covers shaken out of their moth-balls in the box-room would have been riches. But those lovely new things must have been specially *chosen* for me. Life with a bed and a table and two kitchen chairs and some packing-cases *is* rather empty, even if one paints the packing-cases different colours and stains the floor. I've been calculating how long it would be before I could buy a basket chair and whether I should have to get some sort of a carpet at once or go about in bedroom slippers.

Because my landlord came up last night to point out that there was a clause in my lease which laid down that tenants must provide suitable floor-covering, and that walnut stain was not. I thought that hard, as I'd used up three evenings and two pairs of stockings over that floor staining, and stuffed my knees with splinters by crawling furiously from point to point so that the stain would dry evenly. But your magnificent carpet covers everything, particularly the place where I kicked over a pot of vermilion paint intended for a packing case.

My walls were dry too, which was fortunate, as I don't think I could have resisted the temptation to try your curtains against them. I thought that distemper alone would be dull, so I distempered them first, a dull yellow, and then varnished experimentally over the top of it, thinking of the inside of a buttercup. The result is really rather like it and pleasing, but the varnishing was dreadfully difficult. I kept getting stuck when I did the corners and fly-papered myself to the wall behind. But just think of those flame-coloured curtains of yours against it! And the carpet to match! And the grand arm-chairs with their cushions! I rushed wildly out and bought all the daffodils that a surprised old man was pushing home on his barrow. Later they shall stand in copper jugs: just at present they're in jam jars.

Will you come to tea on Sunday to see it all? The flat's quite easy to find. Turn left from the King's Road towards the river. Christchurch Street is on the far side of Tite Street and you can take the car all the way down. My house is the second on the left from the far end, and there's a potted bay tree in the front garden. Also a grocer's opposite with one of these YOU CAN TELEPHONE FROM HERE signs. Such a comfort: from my flat you can't.

Christchurch Street goes on to the river, and that's another advantage, as I walk along the Embankment for miles most evenings after work while I'm waiting for some of the distemper to dry. (But I shan't get painter's colic. The windows are open all the time.)

Ring the bell three times: I'll come down and let you in. With love – and thanks.

HILARY

DAILY REPORT

February 11th, 1932

Health of Staff

In Charge H Fane (Sister Smith's half-day. Miss Ward at Staff Meeting.)

Sick List 2-6 pm. Total 21

Particulars

2.15 Miss Watts required sal volatile.

2.30 Miss Player of the Soft Furnishings asked if she might go home. (Sick.)

2.45 Miss Brown of Silk Lingerie asked for brandy. (Received sal volatile.)

3.0 (onwards.) Administered soda mint to eighteen applicants, most of whom mentioned brandy.

4.0 Four victims able and anxious to go home. Three still lying down. Three back at work.

5.0 Final round of soda mint. All now asking to go home.

Investigation proved:

(1) All victims had lunched in canteen.

(2) All had eaten rabbit pie.

Treatment

I have spoken to cook. She says:

(a) That there was nothing in that pie but the best fresh rabbit and pastry, and a few assorted veg to make it tasty.

(b) It had been cooked in the self-regulating ovens on the premises and to the recipe within a minute.

(c) She was a hard-working woman with a family of five that never ailed anything and a husband what was most particular.

(d) No cooking in the world is proof against gobbling, and if girls would eat their dinner in five minutes because they wanted to go to these rehearsals they're all talking about morning noon and night the best food would turn on them.

Remarks

(1) Only three of the victims performing in staff play, *The Girl Aboard the Lugger*. Which would seem to disallow (d) at least in part.

(2) As there is no pie left and the dishes have been washed, it is impossible to diagnose; but it is probable from evidence obtained that the kitchen maid forgot to put holes in the pastry. This, I understand, has been known to cause severe illness.

(3) Have ventured to put this hypothesis before cook. Not well received.

BUSINESS AS USUAL

EVERYMAN'S STORES

For use in inter-departmental correspondence only

From M E Ward *To* Miss Fane

February 12th, 1932

Subject Yesterday's Daily Report

Memo

Cook seriously offended. Leave her to me in future. Good cooks scarce.

M E WARD

BT/MEW

2A CHRISTCHURCH STREET

February 23rd

DEAREST FAMILY,

D'you remember my writing some time before Christmas about an odd-looking man with a bull terrier who came into the shop and asked for Daddy's book? He reappeared to-day, and stood about demanding to see me till Mr Salt rushed up to my office and brought me away from the young women with degrees whom I was interviewing for posts in the Library.

At first I thought there was going to be trouble. He had that boiling-over expression which means Customer-in-state-of-acute-complaint-and-seeking-victim. And he opened on me at once. He understood my father's new book was out. Yes, it was. Well then? Hadn't he given explicit instructions that it was to be sent to him? So I had to admit that he hadn't given his name and I didn't know it. There was an explosive, contemptuous sort of sound; then he laughed. And gave it to me.

My dears, it was Rutherford Worsthorne; by his own account (later gogglingly confirmed by Mr Salt) one of the rather leading diggers up of antiquity. I said I'd heard a lot about him from Daddy – which was true, but I couldn't remember any of it – promised to make a note – assured him that all future books by Professor Fane should be sent to him on publication. (For pity's sake write another soon!) I did hope that he would accept our … (all the apologetic patter). But he wasn't impressed. He just said, 'Ah, yes. Well, I hadn't come merely to register a protest. Look here, Miss Fane, is there anywhere we can talk?' I said yes but he went right on where he was. 'The thing is – well, are you devoted to commerce?'

I murmured and wondered, and he explained: 'I'm going to Greece this spring with a small party. Want a secretary. Not a chit. Must be a competent creature ...'

All this, my dears, in the very public middle of Everyman's Book Floor, with every ear in the room straining. I eventually managed to lead him away to my office, sent an applicant to wait outside (on that chair I sat on last September) and listened to his ideas.

Greece in the Spring! It sounded marvellous. I don't know why the glamour of that country should have survived a semi-classical education, but it has. Geographically, I believe, it's just a series of bare hills covered with Hellenic travellers and temples with Cook's men behind every column. But my picture of it is full of almond blossom and budding olives, and sheets of asphodel and all Persephone's other flowers climbing up Mount Parnassus.

It might fit in so beautifully too. If Daddy felt like taking his holiday in September this year I could perhaps join you for it when we came home. Oh, this is the maddest talk for a girl who *isn't* going to be married in the autumn, and who's got a really good and responsible job which might Last her a Lifetime with care (and, therefore, doesn't bear thinking about). You see, I want to get out of London rather badly. Mary Meldon likes my flat and wants somewhere to live. She might take it on while we were away, and she and I might share it, perhaps, when I came back. For Mr Worsthorne wants a permanent secretary to dig up Greece and cruise about the islands and record results in the spring and summer, and also to come and work with him in London in the autumn.

Of course there are lots of pros and cons. There'd not be so much money, for one thing. Nor a Career. But it'd be a human existence, with lots of travelling and visible holidays and blessedly variable hours. Nine-to-six still sits on my soul like a tombstone every now and then.

Anyway, he doesn't want a decision just at once. His own plans aren't really settled, and I'm to think it over. Meanwhile, he's asked me to a lecture on Something Hellenic and taking me out to dinner first. A kindly thought, but I shall feel uncomfortably On Appro. And very doubtful of sustaining the family reputation on dinner-table topics.

Do tell me that you don't think this as crazy as it sounds. Castle-jerry-building cheers one up in the middle of an unenterprising existence. Not that mine is without its upheavals. Lots of odd things keep happening, including Words with the canteen cook yesterday and Everyman's Dramatic Society's performance to-morrow night. I'm not letting this vagary 'Unsettle' me. It's just a pleasant thing to have about one's mind.

With lots of love,

HILARY

2A CHRISTCHURCH STREET
CHELSEA

March 6th, 1932

DEAR MR GRANT,

I expect that the officials of the E Orch Soc (in which is incorporated the E A Op Soc and the E D C) are writing on behalf of their organisations to sympathise with you over your accident in general and on missing last night's performance of *The Girl Aboard the Lugger* in particular. I was very sorry to hear about the accident. Rumour variously has it that you have sustained:

(a) A fractured skull

(b) Two broken arms

(c) Hopelessly crushed ribs – with splinters penetrating adjacent vital organs

(d) Compound fracture of the thigh

(e) Water on the knees and the loss of most toes, besides being burnt out of recognition.

Sister Smith says you've sprained an ankle. In either case I should have thought you were to be congratulated on producing such an impressive alibi. I had none to hand when Mr Salt presented me with a ticket, at the same time admitting that he was taking a small part in the performance himself. Which meant, I found, that he was the hero, and playing opposite Miss Morley of the Perfumes and Bath Salts. But as she went down with flu just before the Dress Rehearsal, Miss Landry of A. Select, Book Floor, is having the chance of her life.

'TENTATIVELY CONDUCTED THEM'

As for the play itself, I doubt if an all star cast could have made much out of such an elderly comedy. And I'm sure that no dispassionate outsider could have sat through it as rendered by the E Orch Soc and Co. Fortunately none of us were dispassionate. The small hall, chartered for the occasion, was packed with friends and relations, so that the applause was more or less continuous. Everybody was encored: everybody had bouquets at the end (flowers for the ladies and lovely bottles of Bass tied up with ribbons for the gentlemen).

But three hours of musical comedy came first. The orchestra crawled into their pit at 7.40 for a 7.30 start: Mr Hibbert took up his place in front and tentatively conducted them through the National Anthem.

The orchestra enjoyed the overture very much, but after a while the curtain went up on an appropriate coastal scene; an insecure cliff with an agitated dark-blue back-cloth wagging behind a yellow beach. The chorus were on – ten pirates with sea-boots, sabres and knives in their teeth, and ten dithering village maidens who seemed to try the producer's patience a good deal. The curtain went up in time to give us a marvellous view of his last words to them, but the well-trained audience clapped at sight, the producer charged back into the wings and the chorus plunged into their first song and dance. There was a certain lack of unanimity, but at the end all the pirates threw the girls piratically over their shoulders and staggered off. Which brought down the house. Then came the spotlight and Mr Salt, completely at his ease, though he rather upset the other actors by introducing a series of entirely irrelevant jokes, learnt up since the Dress Rehearsal and sprung on an unsuspecting cast. All the young women giggled and there was a sort of prolonged growling from the O P corner.

At one point I had hopes that the producer would emerge and fall upon Mr Salt. Some of his curses coincided with a pianissimo bit for the orchestra, and Mr Hibbert was so startled that he dropped his baton. After that one half of the orchestra ran away with the other, and kept the lead to the end of that number, in spite of everything Mr Hibbert, wild and weaponless, could do.

Miss Landry, of course, dried up at the first unrehearsed item. But she got her own back during the spot-lit love duet, which hardly left a dry parental eye in the house. Mr Salt's thin tenor hadn't a chance against her soprano, particularly as she managed (I hope by accident) to get a thumb on his windpipe during an embrace, and eventually tripped him up with his own sword.

But the event of the evening was the Pirates' Hornpipe in the last act, even though make-up and performers had begun to wilt a bit by then. The Pirates' costumes had been rather odd from the beginning, of course. I don't know how one hires clothes for a chorus, but does one procure them by the dozen and then go round counting them out with, 'Out-size, stock-size, medium large? ...'

The result looked like it. But the sea-boots were all tremendous, so that the dancers looked apprehensive. Some people's corns made it dangerous for them to keep their feet on the ground and other people's boots would have dropped off if they'd lifted them, so that there was no particular unanimity there either, except between the hero and heroine who appeared forgivingly on board the lugger and kissed throughout.

After that the audience kept the curtain seesawing up and down for about ten minutes while sections of the cast appeared or fled in embarrassment or dragged others on or were caught alone by accident in the centre of the stage, according to disposition. I saw the flowers and bottles delivered, then crept out, with my ears buzzing and walked home along the Embankment.

Anyone reported to have concussion or a fractured skull was quite definitely better in bed. But, talking of concussion, what about those library reports? Shall I take them to somebody else? Or wait? Or post them to you? Things are going rather well now. Having done all she can to wreck the new system, Miss Sparling has convinced herself that it originally emanated from her and that she is being defrauded of all credit. As this belief seems to please her, perhaps it's all for the best.

One's not to know, of course, when she may become homicidal again. I hope you're a quick mender.

Yours sincerely,

HILARY FANE

2A CHRISTCHURCH STREET
CHELSEA

March 9th, 1932

DEAR MR GRANT,

Thank you for your note. I'm glad you liked the unofficial account of the Staff Play. I'm also and more glad that you liked the drawings. People mostly don't, or at least they don't mention them, which is worse I think on the whole.

Herewith the estimates for redecorating the extension of the Library. I got three, which don't vary substantially, except that one seems more comprehensive than the others. In the meantime I've been getting on with the minor innovations, such as knocking down the wall which used to separate us from the Baby Linen Department (now removing in extreme displeasure to the annexe on the third floor).

That extra floor and shelf space is going to be a godsend, and quite worth the interview I had with Mrs Barlow, the dispossessed buyer. The new desks are in and the new shelves in course of construction. I've controlled the scheme rather carefully, so that the department has never been entirely out of action at any time, though the assistants have been harried by workmen and exasperated by carpenter noises for the last week.

Miss Sparling sits at her desk refusing to move herself or her papers under a rain of sawdust and small tools. You know that sort of obstinate, unnecessary infuriating heroism.

Most of the others are visibly intrigued, and the new, alphabetically placarded desks have been greatly admired. I explained that subscribers would now change their books according to the initial syllable of their surnames, not according to the sort of subscription they can afford. Even a Fiction C subscription can now be taken out without contumely. I'm sure that's likely to swell the numbers, besides being a humane innovation. It's so pleasant to have one's humble order treated with the same deference as one given by the lady with the sables and the Rolls.

I've also engaged half a dozen rather well equipped and beautiful clerks to staff my desks. I've set my heart on raising the standard of librarians to the level of the *Daily Post Book Guild's* young women. No one without a title or a degree need apply. Subscribers do appreciate good diners-out.

May I know, at your convenience, how far I may go with my schemes? Do you like the idea of a row of cases of rare bindings and first editions and book-plates? I think it might fire the mere library fans to Own Books, and urge them towards the shop.

Yours sincerely,

HILARY FANE

2A CHRISTCHURCH STREET
CHELSEA

March 11th

DEAR AUNT BERTHA,

I'm dreadfully sorry, but I shan't be able to come to tea this Saturday after all. It's business, of course. But not really sweated labour, so please don't take any presidential notice of it. It just happens that we're instituting some alterations and reforms on the Book Floor at Everyman's, and Mr Grant, my immediate superior, is pinned to his sofa with a sprained ankle and other incidental damage. We both want the alterations to go through without any delay, and see eye to eye in the way that none of the economical old gentlemen on the Board would be likely to, as they're handicapped by an enormous respect for the present state of affairs.

I've been getting reports ready, so that I can have them approved and put into action first thing Monday morning, and Mr Grant has summoned me to appear at his flat with them. You do appreciate that that sort of royal command isn't to be taken lightly, don't you? I'm very sorry to miss your tea-party, and Trades Union annoyed at having to work on Saturday afternoon.

That's what comes of not being quite a hireling, of course. You can't always leave the work to look after itself over the week-end. But Mr Grant is rather a brilliant person, with infectious enthusiasms. I wonder if Uncle Tom knows him? He represents Everyman's on the United Purveyors' Council, I believe. So they may have met.

I do hope you understand about Saturday, and will forgive

me. Perhaps I might come in for half an hour on my way home instead?

Yours affectionately,

HILARY

2A CHRISTCHURCH STREET

March 12th
Saturday evening

DEAREST FAMILY,

Thank you *very* much for the nice, familiar chairs. Are you sure that you can spare the one from the library? I shall love to have them, though I'm sorry you didn't like the idea of those packing-cases. Perhaps it's all for the best, though. What with your contributions and Aunt Bertha's astonishing gift of assorted furnishings Mrs Bland's confidence is quite restored. Especially since she's been allowed to break up the painted packing-cases and lay the sittingroom fire with them. They're wonderful for getting it going, though they smell rather during conflagration.

And I was glad to have your temperate letter about Greece and Rutherford Worsthorne. I'm still dithering towards the idea, but I've been so busy at Everyman's that I've only been able to take it out in crowded buses where it seems like heaven, and just before going to sleep when it seems a very Momentous Step. No decision so far. Tremendous reconstructions are going on in the Library, and all sorts of calculations and correspondence and continual reports are involved. In the absence of Mr Grant (post-motor accident) I've been coping with these entirely. And I've had to bring sheaves of papers home in the evenings to work at till all hours. Mrs Bland came in to wash up after supper and found the sitting-room snow-drifted with them. She said: 'Dear me, miss, you have been busy. But of course you're always littry.' Now, which do *you* think she meant?

But it's really been rather fearsomely responsible work, so I was glad as well as astonished when I was bidden to bring my reports to Mr Grant's flat on Saturday afternoon, overtime though it was. He has one of those nice bachelor flats that look over the park, and I expected him to be laid out on a sofa. But he was at the top of a library ladder in his study, reaching down books, with one foot bandaged and dangling in a bedroom slipper, and a gorgeous grey Persian cat was sharpening its claws against one of the brown leather arm-chairs.

He said, 'Good-afternoon,' very stately; but on second thoughts asked me to hold the ladder while he got down. After that I produced my papers and we talked business besottedly for an hour and a half. He has an immense, and most alarming appetite for detail: his mind grabs each fact and swallows it whole while mine grasshoppers from point to point. By the time I had proved my conclusions and he had approved my schemes I was worn to a thread. But his man wheeled in restoratives; tea and buttered toast and a very solid cake, just in time.

The cat had kept its distance till then, but as I was asking about cream and sugar two stone of grey tom-Persian landed disconcertingly on my lap. Mr Grant said: 'Push that thing off if it annoys you.' But I was much too flattered to disturb it, though it was thoughtfully kneading the shape out of my new spring suit. We spent a very restful hour, just eating and smoking, and talking about mice and psycho-analysis and Walt Disney and chair covers and Spiritualism and Black Magic (he has some enthralling books on witchcraft). Just as I was going he said it was so good of me to have sacrificed a whole precious afternoon of free time to business. He'd like to arrange something to repay us both – a dinner and theatre, he thought. Did I agree?

So we fixed a date, rather far ahead, as he said he doubted if he'd be an adequate escort for three weeks at least. What festivities! I've got to go to another Hellenic lecture on Tuesday week.

On my way home I called on Aunt Bertha. Since I'd missed her tea-party I thought it might be a tactful thing to do. So I received her sympathy for my hard afternoon's work quite heroically. It seems that Uncle Tom knows Michael Grant slightly – which may be dangerous. I hope that Aunt Bertha won't attempt any of her machinations for my preferment at Everyman's.

But she was very sweet, though obviously on the verge of a party and preoccupied about what to wear. I didn't stay long, and took away all sorts of messages and love to you – the sort that wants acknowledging, I rather think. Do write.

It's raining: I shall slither out to post this, and then go to bed, very conscious of my day's work. And I shall stay there All To-morrow.

With lots of love,

HILARY

PART III – SPRING

CHRISTCHURCH STREET

March 22nd

DEAREST FAMILY,

Just a note. I'm feeling harried. I came in from my Hellenic lecture which was (saving your presence, Professor) quite gruesomely dull, to find an incredibly monogrammed invitation card waiting for me. From Aunt Bertha! It's one of her most stupendous dinners at which decorations are to be worn. Me, of all poor relations! I can't think what's possessed her.

But as she's chosen the same night as Michael Grant I think I ought to refuse for the sake of my Career, on the same principle as I attend Hellenic lectures. I shall have to tell Aunt Bertha that I'm going away for the week-end. Nothing else sounds adequate. I thought I'd better let you know at once, so that if you'd not written already you wouldn't commit yourselves about my doings.

Love,

HILARY

BUSINESS AS USUAL

EVERYMAN'S STORES

For use in inter-departmental correspondence only

From H Fane *To* Staff Supervisor
March 26th, 1932

Subject Ventilation in the Clerical Department, Book Floor

Memo

In accordance with your memo of yesterday's date, I have investigated this, and the following facts emerge.

There are five windows: all are closed.

The general opinion approves of this: though

Miss Dowland says she likes fresh air, and would sooner have a window open even if she had to wear two of everything in consequence.

Miss Watts won't have her window open because she's so subject to rheumatism, and if I'd ever tried to type with a real stiff neck running down both arms I'd know how awkward it could be.

Miss Hopper won't have *her* window open because she suffers with her stomach, and the least thing gives her a chill on it. And

Mr Simpson says that once people go opening these windows he'll have trouble with his bronchs all spring. He knows just how it'll be. It isn't that he minds for himself at all, but he's often noticed the way Ventilation takes all the good out of Heating, and it wouldn't do for the typists to be cold. As it is, Mr Millett lets in far too much cold air, opening and shutting the door the way he does.

Miss Lamb has chilblains.

I have told Mr Millett to keep the door shut and got the carpenter to open one window. Suggested a muffler to Miss Watts, a body belt to Miss Dowland, changed Miss Hopper's seat, advised Miss Lamb to take an iron tonic and offered thermogene to Mr Simpson.

Looked in two hours later. Window closed. Doubt if it is likely to remain open unless fixed; with nails.

Please advise.

H FANE

THE FLAT

April 1st

DEAREST MUMMY AND DADDY,

Easter was marvellous. I didn't go into details of my plans beforehand, as I felt that you would be unlikely to show any pronounced enthusiasm at the idea of Mary Meldon and me cruising across England in a car which Mary had just bought for £10. Now that we're safely home without a bruise between us I can enlarge.

The car hadn't much hood, only one door and no paint whatever. I was rather shaken myself at first sight of Mary's Colossal Bargain, but she said: 'My good girl, don't *look*. Listen. She's ticking over like a Daimler.' We tried her out on the Great West Road after work and came home babbling with excitement at her behaviour. As Mary said, one could always take the worse hills (up or down) in reverse. Though actually we only had to do that twice.

We wrangled a bit about destination beforehand. Mary said Wales and I said Yorkshire, so we had to go to Devonshire instead. We left at six o'clock on Thursday – like everybody else, unfortunately – and came back proudly from Salisbury alone and at sunrise on Tuesday morning.

It rained a good deal, but we reinforced that hood with a waterproof sheet and enjoyed ourselves triumphantly, though the car drank as much oil as petrol, which began to come expensive. After the first hundred miles the springs sagged a good deal, and one mudguard broke loose and flapped. All the young men on motor cycles putt-putted up to us and craned their necks to Point it Out before they streaked off in front. Also there were streams of obese motor buses carting people in paper hats to the sea. 'Hell's Delights!' said Mary, and systematically passed them on corners.

We walked a lot on Sunday and Monday, barelegged with sandshoes, which is, believe me, the only way of walking in Devon at Easter. The return journey was queer and exciting: the first villages were all asleep (and it's startling to know how few people open windows even in 1932), the next had a few postmen and labourers wheeling out bicycles: then there were milk bottles and newspapers on doorsteps, and London finally was broad awake.

Tuesday, of course, was just the longest day I've lived through, though I only went to sleep once, quite discreetly, in my office. But I had to keep going up to the Canteen for large black coffees. Still, a success. Mary's going to farm out the car to a young man who wants to take round samples and will garage it till Whitsun. Then we've promised ourselves the Lakes, even Edinburgh if I could get the Saturday morning off and we could drive all night. What do you think?

By the way, you'll be interested to know that Mr Worsthorne has made up his mind about Greece. He reappeared yesterday with all his plans cut and dried, and wanted my decision At Once.

I said no. Always the best answer in an emergency. And much less disruptive. I suddenly and surprisingly felt that I couldn't bear to leave London. After all the fuss I've been making about travel and holidays and congenial work too! Stability instead of adventure – how are the mighty fallen. That sort of mad-rabbiting across Europe sounds so marvellous, but it doesn't seem to lead anywhere. I was very apologetic and threw him Mary Meldon's address as a sop. But he went away muttering.

So here I am, settled down for the summer. I must look out for some striped sun-blinds for the flat. It ought to be easy: Everyman's Garden Accessories department shows everything from snail-traps to statues.

I can't write more now; I've just got time for a bath before I go out to dinner with Michael Grant.

Much love to you both,

HILARY

PS – 'Nothing canst thou to damnation add greater than this!' Shakespeare's profanity, not mine. But applicable. What an evening! It began beautifully too. I do so appreciate dining in public with an expert, and Michael was entirely charming –quite unofficial. We set out for Drury Lane purring companionably.

Then things began to happen. My dears, just as we were sidling into our stalls I looked up and was Transfixed by the sight of Aunt Bertha's party constellated in the Stage Box. I very nearly died, but just managed to keep my chin down, praying that she wouldn't recognise the top of my head. We enjoyed the first act. But in the interval Michael said happily: 'Hallo, there's Lady Barnley. I should have been dining with her to-night if you hadn't provided an alibi!'

Of course I saw the whole thing! I knew that Aunt Bertha *would* machinate for my betterment, but I never dreamed that Michael, offered a chance of meeting quite as many potentates, would so honourably refuse. And you know how touchy Aunt Bertha is!

In my panic I looked up and found her astonished lorgnettes full on us. My one idea was instant and abject flight with a vague idea of the next train north, but Michael made me stay and insisted on supper afterwards, which saved the evening.

Will you kindly tell me – *what* does the victim do next?

H

2A CHRISTCHURCH STREET
CHELSEA

April 2nd

DEAR MICHAEL,

I went round to Cadogan Square this afternoon to explain about last night. Aunt Bertha was hurt. She couldn't see why either of us should seriously consider the other a 'previous social engagement of long standing' when invited to the sort of Dinner where Decorations were to be Worn. Especially when I had made things worse by saying that I was to be away for the week-end.

It was all a little unfortunate, particularly since I refused a Saturday tea-party in the rather immediate past because you had commanded an audience. I talked and talked. She said, quite reasonably, that I should have told her who was taking me out instead of 'making such a mystery of it'. Then we'd have found out that we'd meet each other at her dinner. As intended. And young men don't have a chance of talking to the President of the Board of Industry every night, not to mention Uncle Tom and a Cabinet Minister. (Oh, Michael, what *have* I done!) Just as I was saying to myself that Aunt Bertha might be so useful, carefully handled, too! I'd even thrown out little suggestions which I hoped might get you invited to some of her dull, grand parties. Then she spontaneously gives an invitation and I wreck it all. Why didn't you tell me? We'd have changed our day. I *do* understand the importance of dining out among the great.

But I think it's more or less all right now. Except that we're to go to dinner on Saturday – 'just ourselves. So nice'. I'm afraid that nothing will recall that Cabinet Minister or the President of the Board of Industry. Do you think your career is shattered? As for Saturday, I think I ought to sacrifice the evening, but I'm quite willing to be offered up alone if you can think of any excuse now likely to carry conviction.

I've apologised too much in the last few minutes to be capable of expressing any further regrets. But I'm miserably conscious of having completely mismanaged things, though I enjoyed our evening, with its alarums and lovely, extravagant supper at midnight quite enormously all the same.

Yours,

HILARY

> 2A CHRISTCHURCH STREET
> CHELSEA
>
> *April 5th*

DEAR MICHAEL,

How noble of you not to mind about that Cabinet Minister. I am so relieved, and even looking forward to Saturday at Aunt Bertha's. Of course you may come and cook sausages over my gas ring another night to make up. What about Thursday?

Even if you feel that you just can't bear to come on Saturday, and think of some brilliant excuse at the last minute, I'll still expect you on Thursday evening, at the flat.

Decorations unnecessary.

> Yours ever,
>
> HILARY

2A CHRISTCHURCH STREET
CHELSEA

April 7th, 1932

MICHAEL DEAR,

It's been such an incredible evening that I can't bring myself to go to bed and end it. Because to-morrow, of course, you'll be just an important official of Everyman's and I'll be an unimportant one. So I want to write to you while the last few hours are still real.

I'm glad about this evening: glad that you've seen my flat and like it: I'm glad you like me: I'm glad and amazed and proud that you want to marry me. Only, you must look in my personal cupboard first. Not that there's much of a skeleton in it – just one of those muddles. But you ought to have an inventory.

I should have pulled myself together to give it three hours ago, when you first began to talk about me, on the Embankment. But I was so surprised and it was so easy just to listen that I didn't protest. I just walked and turned, and walked and turned with you beside that parapet, and didn't say a word. As you know. But now, listen. I was engaged until two months ago, and it wasn't a success. I exasperated a nice, clever man into being unkind to me, and then broke off the engagement. Which was grossly unfair and feminine. I didn't even know that I was being exasperating and obstinate – that's what's so frightening.

It all happened because I insisted on spending the year before we could be married earning my living in London. I refused to give in and come home when I was told, or when things went badly here. That was after the library investigations that you organised. What a mercy you did, by the way. If I'd still been a label-writer it couldn't have happened. At least, not happily. You might have made a marvellous King Cophetua, but I'd never be a queenly beggarmaid. I'm too Scots: always folding my hands and knowing my place.

I don't mean that because things went wrong last time that they'd be bound to go wrong again. I think this is different, but will you understand if I ask you to wait a while? Not for a year: I don't think I could bear it. But leave things as they are for six months. We won't be engaged: we'll see each other as usual. It'll be odd, but it'll be good to know that you're in the same town, the same building; to come back every morning to a chance of meeting you. And then, whatever we find at the end of the six months; whether it's been a whim and died, or a real relationship that's going to survive, you've made me very happy for one evening by telling me.

Yours – *faithfully*,

HILARY

Private. Not to be filed.

EVERYMAN'S STORES

For use in inter-departmental correspondence only

From Michael Grant *To* Hilary Fane
October 7th, 1932

Subject Your letter of April 7th

Memo

With reference to the proposal made six months ago; this seems now due for further consideration.

In the event of your reaching a favourable decision, do you authorise me to obtain the necessary paraphernalia?

M G G

BUSINESS AS USUAL

Private. Not to be filed.

EVERYMAN'S STORES
For use in inter-departmental correspondence only

From Hilary Fane   *To* Michael Grant
                                 October 7th, 1932

Subject Your memo of this morning's date.

Memo

I do.

                                                                   H F

Notes on the novel

BY KATE MACDONALD

Part I – Autumn

FRCS: Fellow of the Royal College of Surgeons

Government House: Basil is from a family in the diplomatic service.

hysterotomy: an incision in the uterus. It's possible that the authors meant 'hysterectomy'.

miniatory: menacing, aggressive.

GFS: Girls' Friendly Society, a charitable organisation designed to care for girls and young women by offering moral precepts and practical help and facilities for work and leisure.

flags: flagstones, a larger, squarer and better quality stone for street paving than cobbles.

distemper: a short-lived undercoat paint used for a cheap decorative treatment.

get off the rails: the trolley-buses ran on rails and were powered by electricity through cables above the roadway, rather like a modern tram system. If a cart wheel got stuck in the rails, there would be an inconvenient hold-up.

chars, or dailies: women who worked as a daily cleaner with some light cooking in more affluent households.

a Pit: a ticket for the theatre, in the area between the stalls and the stage, and one of the cheapest seats in the house.

Home Chat: a weekly magazine for working women and girls, with recipes, home hints, puzzles, an advice column and serial stories.

Lyons: a famous chain of tea-shops.

Dining Rooms: licensed inexpensive restaurants for a working clientele, with a set menu.

County Council: Mr Millett went to a state school, possibly on a County Council scholarship, rather than the fee-paying schools that Hilary and Basil would have attended.

Night School: adult evening classes in subjects designed to help working men, and women, who had not been able to go to college to advance in their careers.

that count: Mr Millett wears clothes emulating those of the typical Cambridge undergraduate.

Trinity: Mr Salt attended Trinity College Cambridge, but dresses as a typical businessman in the City.

ABC: another chain of tea-shops.

mountains: How beautiful on the mountains are the feet of him who brings good news. Isaiah 52.7.

annunciatory: the Annunciation was the Virgin being given the news that she was to bear the son of God. Mr Simpson must have looked similarly beatific.

Eno's: Eno's Fruit Salts, a fizzy tablet to add to water, a long-standing indigestion remedy.

Fiction C: circulating libraries had different levels of book offered to customers depending on their subscription. C would have been the oldest set of stock, which would have been in circulation for some time, and the books would have looked well-read.

corres: correspondence.

par: paragraph.

Anglo-Indian way: excessively concerned about social status, and probably fiercely racist.

japanned: a lacquered finish on wood or other friable surfaces.

wash-stand: a stand containing a china bowl in a recess, and possibly also a space for a jug of hot water. The Colonel's wife would wash herself here, so it was an intimate space to be screened from public view.

divan: a flat bed with no headboard or footboard, that could be disguised as a sofa in a room used for day as well as night.

area: Georgian and Victorian London houses typically had a paved area outside the basement door or window, which lighted the basement rooms, usually the kitchens.

lacrimae rerum: the tears of things, from Book I of the *Aeneid*.

hot-bottle: hot-water bottle.

Turn again Whittington: from the legend of Dick Whittington, thrice Mayor of London.

White Knight: an impressive but day-dreaming character, from Lewis Carroll's *Alice Through the Looking-Glass*.

carbons: carbon-treated paper sheets to ensure that the writing on the page will be copied automatically onto the page below.

Deil take the hindmost: Scots saying, that the devil will take the last in the race, or, every man for himself.

Palmerston: the shop uses a code with a key to ensure that customers can't work out the prices of the books. P = 1, A = 2, L = 3, and so on.

Marie Stopes: author of books about contraception and sexual advice for couples, written from a medical and psychological perspective. She was a notorious name, the founder of the Marie Stopes family planning clinics and also a best-selling author.

beagles and the Cam: Mr Salt evidently used to go out with the beagles, ie run alongside dogs when hunting, and rowed on the Cam while at Cambridge.

leathercraft and string: this suggests that the slightly impoverished readers of Fiction C books went in for leather handicrafts at evening classes and knitted their own shopping bags, which would not have been at all fashionable.

benzine: although considered a dangerous chemical now, benzene, also a fuel, is a solvent, and was used as a rapid cleaning agent to remove stains in some fabrics. It is also flammable, as Hilary found out.

perilously: parquet wood flooring can be lethally slippery if polished with wax too enthusiastically.

Society papers: magazines like the *Graphic*, *Tatler*, *Horse and Hound*, *Country Life*, with more photographs of Society people at play than text.

Pig won't get over the Stile: from the folk tale 'The Old Woman and her Pig'.

Part II – Winter

Upper Circle: a more expensive seat at the theatre than a Pit (see above).

larn: learn, from the dialect phrase 'that'll larn ye', ie 'that'll teach you'.

pi-dog: Anglo-Indian term for pariah dog, a homeless scavenger.

promiscuous: she doesn't feel like seeing lots of people.

sedentary beams: wide bottoms that don't get much exercise. Hiking, rather than simply going for a walk, was becoming very popular in the 1930s.

Christian: from Bunyan's *The Pilgrim's Progress*.

Roman Holiday: an event where the spectators take pleasure in watching another's suffering.

Irish Sweep: The Irish Free State Hospitals Lottery was a fundraising lottery set up in the Republic of Ireland in 1930 to raise money for its hospitals, and sold tickets with the names of horses running in various Irish and British races. Lotteries were at that time illegal in the UK, so it was very popular among British betters. Mixing Day may have been the day when the tickets were separated and mixed into the different drums used to sell the Sweepstake tickets on the streets.

teeth out: aside from dental health not being high in people with poor nutrition, it was routine in the early part of the twentieth century to have one's teeth removed as a prospective cure for physical problems elsewhere in the body, as well as to remove them before painful abscesses could set in.

tumbler: false teeth were routinely kept in a tumbler of water beside the bed, so the teeth could be taken out discreetly at night and popped back in in the morning.

ex-officio: by virtue of her office.

frogged: frog-kick swimming.

in trouble: Miss Lamb was pregnant, and unmarried, which was a serious social and civic catastrophe: this would lose her her job, and she would have to keep the baby's existence, or her lack of a husband, secret to get future work.

flitting: the process of moving house.

pantechnicon: a very large removals lorry.

Part III – Spring

E Orch Soc: variously, the Everyman's Orchestral Society, the Everyman's Amateur Operatic Society and the Everyman's Dramatic Company.

O P corner: stands for 'opposite prompt corner', referring to the traditional location for the prompter in a play, seated at stage left. Thus O P is stage right.

contumely: feeling humiliated.

More Handheld Classics

Rediscover some of our other Classics about women's stories and urban lives from the early twentieth century.

What Not:
A Prophetic Comedy
by Rose Macaulay

What Not is Rose Macaulay's speculative novel of post-First World War eugenics and newspaper manipulation that influenced Aldous Huxley's *Brave New World*.

Published in 1918, *What Not* was hastily withdrawn due to a number of potentially libellous pages, and was reissued in 1919, but had lost its momentum. Republished in 2019 with the suppressed pages reinstated for the first time, *What Not* is a lost classic of feminist protest at social engineering, and rage at media manipulation.

Kitty Grammont and Nicholas Chester are in love. Kitty is certified as an A for breeding purposes, but politically ambitious Chester has been uncertificated, and may not marry. Kitty wields power as a senior civil servant in the Ministry of Brains, which makes these classifications, but she does not have the freedom to marry who she wants. They ignore the restrictions, and carry on a discreet affair. But it isn't discreet enough for the media: the popular press, determined to smash the brutal regime of the Ministry of Brains, has found out about Kitty and Chester, and scents an opportunity for a scandalous exposure.

Aldous Huxley was a frequent guest at Macaulay's flat while she was writing *What Not*. Fourteen years later, his *Brave New World* borrowed many of Macaulay's ideas for Huxley's own prophetic vision.

The introduction is by Sarah Lonsdale, Senior Lecturer in journalism at City University London.

Save Me The Waltz
by Zelda Fitzgerald

Zelda Fitzgerald's only novel, *Save Me The Waltz* (1932) was written in six weeks and covers the period of her life that her husband F Scott Fitzgerald had been drawing on for years while writing *Tender is the Night* (1934). She died in 1948. *Save Me The Waltz* is now recognised as a classic novel of the woman's experience in fast-moving American Jazz Age society.

The novel opens during the First World War. Alabama Beggs is a Southern belle who makes her début into adulthood with wild parties, dancing and drinking, and flirting with the young officers posted to her home town. When the artist Lieutenant David Knight arrives to join her line of suitors, Alabama marries him. Their life in New York, Paris and the South of France closely mirrors the Fitzgeralds' own life and their prominent socialising in the 1920s and 1930s as part of what was later called the Lost Generation.

Like Zelda, Alabama became passionate about dance. She attends ballet class in Paris every day. She refuses to accept that she might not become the great dancer that she ardently longs to be, and this threatens her mental health and her marriage.

The introduction to the novel by Erin E Templeton, Professor of English at Converse College, shows how these struggles to become a dancer were the result of Zelda's need to have a life of her own rather than living in her husband's shadow.

Blitz Writing: Night Shift & It Was Different At The Time

by Inez Holden

Emerging out of the 1940–1941 London Blitz, the drama of these two short works, a novel and a memoir, comes from the courage and endurance of ordinary people met in the factories, streets and lodging houses of a city under bombardment.

Inez Holden's novella *Night Shift* follows a largely working-class cast of characters for five night shifts in a factory that produces camera parts for war planes.

It Was Different At The Time is Holden's account of wartime life from April 1938 to August 1941, drawn from her own diary. This was intended to be a joint project written with her friend George Orwell (he was in the end too busy to contribute), and includes disguised appearances by notable literary figures of the period.

The experiences recorded in *It Was Different At The Time* overlap in period and subject with *Night Shift*, setting up a vibrant dialogue between the two texts.

Inez Holden (1903-1974) was a British writer and literary figure whose social and professional connections embraced most of London's literary and artistic life. She modelled for Augustus John, worked alongside Evelyn Waugh, and had close relationships with George Orwell, Stevie Smith, H G Wells, Cyril Connolly, and Anthony Powell.

The introduction and notes are by Kristin Bluemel, Professor of English at Monmouth University, New Jersey.